SHADOW
PRISON

Dark Fae Paranormal Prison Series

Book One

G. BAILEY
SCARLETT SNOW

Formatting by Champagne Book Design
www.champagnebookdesign.com

Proofread by Becky Edits, www.facebook.com/beckyedits2

The shadows are my prison… and I can't escape.

I'm Izora Dawn, and I've been locked away for something I didn't do. But that's what they all say, right?

When rumoured only the dangerous survive Shadowborn Prison, I know I have no choice but to fight for my life. Luckily my short time at Shadowborn Academy, home to those with dark magic seducing their souls, has taught me how to do just that.

Survival is what I'm known for in this world.

Seduction is what I'm best at.

I figure the quickest way to escape this prison is by seducing the sexy new governor. With a handsome Shadow Warden watching my every move, an alpha inmate eager to protect me, and a hunky teacher from the academy desperate to free me…I might actually get out of this alive.

But in the shadows lie secrets that hold the walls of this prison together.

And no one can escape them.

Not even me.

Shadowborn Prison is a crossover spin-off to Shadowborn Academy. You do not need to read the latter to follow this series. One is for sure—not even the shadows can be trusted in this Enchanted Forest… 18+ Reverse Harem Dark Fae Prison Romance.

THE ENCHANTED FOREST MAP

LEGEND KEY

⚓ Aurora Bay	🜨 Wishing Well	🔒 Shadowborn Prison
🏛 Helios Academy	⚖ Fountain of Mene	🏛 Shadowborn Academy
🏚 Pegasus Inn	🜔 Devil's Drop	
🜹 Zorya Inn	▣ Black Harbour	

"Freedom lies in being bold."
—*Robert Frost*

PREFACE

Created by the Zorya Sisters, Selena and Danica, goddesses of the Moon and Sun, the *Enchanted Forest* is a
realm where darkness thrives and light casts the biggest
shadows of all. It's also where shadowborns are ostracised,
kingdoms fight for dominance, and the Dark and Light
Fae play wicked games. The rules here are not for mortals—they're for those with magic in their souls and darkness in their hearts…

PROLOGUE

"**D**O YOU KNOW THE DIFFERENCE BETWEEN light and dark fae, little one?"

The man towers over me, his face covered by the shadows lurking within the room. A panicked reaction grips me as I try to recall who the gruff voice belongs to and why I can taste blood on my lips. *Where in the name of Selena am I?* The stabbing pain in my head feels like someone has split my skull open, forcing my thoughts to pour out and leaving only hazy remnants. One moment, I was at Shadowborn Academy, partying with my friends who won this year's Tryouts, and the next...darkness.

I try to move my arms, but they're strapped down beside me on the metal table. I kick my legs out, but they, too, are trapped. My heart thrashes against my ribcage as I struggle to move or recall anything beyond the fleeting glimmers in my mind. What the hell happened? And who the *fuck* is this creep leering down at me?

"I know that the light... and dark fae... are all bat-shit crazy," I scream at him, fruitlessly trying to break the bonds, "and I want nothing to do with them!"

I twist my body like a fish swept onto the sand. The leather straps merely cut into my wrists and ankles, and someone else chuckles in the darkness. An icy shiver snakes down the length of my spine. I shoot my eyes around the room, seeing nothing in the inky blackness but sensing more than one pair of eyes on me. The scent of bleach and an inexplicable sweetness invades my senses. It clings to the back of my throat and stings my eyes.

"Let me go! Let me go, you twisted fuckers!"

A blinding light pierces my eyes, blocking out the person above.

"The difference between light and dark fae," he answers in an almost droning voice, "is that a light fae cannot be simply created. Light fae are said to be only born and they are the true creatures of magic. Dark fae can be easily made from a human or shadowborn with an evil heart."

Everyone in the forest knows this, so why is he telling me?

"Telling the poor girl fairytales isn't going to make this easier," a smooth, deep voice replies, right before a door slams shut.

I flinch at the booming noise across the room.

"I guess you're right." The man leans back, his shadow blinking in the light. "But she isn't just any girl, and I suspect she will survive this treatment. Won't you, Izora? I will be disappointed if you die on me. I've researched your

2

bloodline long enough that I am certain you should survive this and become something incredible. Are you ready to be reborn, little one?"

Reborn? Die? Bloodline? My head swims with the words.

"What are you going to do to me?" I choke out, a tinge of fear crawling up my throat, threatening to strangle me. I summon my dark magic, the magic I've trained for years to learn to control, but nothing happens.

True panic kicks in, snatching the air from my lungs, and the fear tightens its grip. I let out a strangled scream and continue to thrash despite my inability to move. A hand presses down hard on my chest, pinning me to the table, while another yanks my head to the side to expose my neck. A sharp needle pricks my nape. I snap my gaze up, delving into a pair of gleaming green eyes. Those eyes are all I remember once the pain takes over.

My bones break and shatter, my heart clenches, my lungs clamp together, and my veins pulse with an agony that is like nothing I have ever felt before. It's like every little part of my body is being ripped open and shredded apart. I scream until my throat gives way, and then I silently beg for death. I beg for my parents to save me. I beg for Selena, the Goddess of the Moon, to spare me.

But no one comes, and the pain doesn't stop.

My heart thrums in my ears like a train racing off the tracks, louder and faster, about to explode under all of the pressure. And then power like I've never known surges into my body, filling me with warmth. A blinding white

3

light shines around me, and a smile touches my lips as all the bindings holding me down disintegrate into dust.

I sit up, looking around at the six males in the room, each of them wearing lab coats.

The one who was leaning over me steps back, his eyes glazed with tears of joy.

"You're a light fae," he says, seizing his colleague's arm. "It worked. It finally worked!"

The pain I felt before is now gone, replaced by a growing strength that heals every torn vessel in my body. I feel like I'm trapped in a dream as I slowly turn my head to see the most breathtaking white wings fluttering behind me. Their beauty is almost otherworldly, and they feel so utterly natural and painless attached to me. It's like they've always been there. Always been a part of my being, rooted in my soul.

Entranced by their beauty, I reach out to touch them. The snowy feathers are like silk between my fingers. So beautiful. But why... why did they do this to me?

I don't notice Green Eyes approaching me. It's not until he places a hand on my shoulder and everything in the room turns nuclear white. The walls crack and tumble and the floor caves into the earth. Dust invades my senses, and the sharp copper tang of blood infiltrates the air, but not once do I feel any pain or sense the blood is my own. It's like the whole world is crumbling at my feet. And yet, I can see the moon, so beautiful, so close, nestled in the inky-black sky. Only then do I let myself fall, praying that the goddess herself will catch me.

CHAPTER ONE

Izora

"THIS IS THE ONE?"

"That's her, all right, sir," the guard replies, his keys clanging as he opens the metal gates outside my cell. Only the small, barred window lets me know I'm still in the Enchanted Forest, the place that has been my home since I was born. Mortals can't find it. Only the fae and magics of this world know of its existence. It's where I belong, and I never want to leave.

I press my back to the padded white wall and shield my gaze from the light I know is about to assault me. The second they open the door, the blinding light claws through my skull and I shriek, cowering away. The light is excruciating and unbearable. I haven't seen anyone since they brought me to this cell. Usually, they just open the door to deliver a tray of food. I have no recollection of what happened before I was brought here, and it annoys me to no end. My last memory is being at Shadowborn Academy, dancing and drinking with my friends and having the time of my life. The next, I'm waking up here, handcuffed and alone.

My pulse spikes as I watch the guards approach me. One of them is a Shadow Warden going by the badge pinned to his coat. The silver buttons running down his chest in two symmetric lines catch the light. I've learned not to strike out at any of Shadow Wardens here as it never ends well. This is the first one I've seen wearing Zorya's black military uniform, complete with the raven cloak pinned around his neck with a wolf-shaped silver brooch.

"Watch out, sir. She's feisty," the guard warns his superior, easing toward me with his taser stick outstretched.

The Shadow Warden's shrewd eyes narrow on my face. "Not with me, she won't be." He crosses his arms and peers down his hooked nose at me. "Here's what's gonna happen, sweetheart. I'm gonna take you from this shitty little room. If you fight me, it'll be the last thing you ever do, you hear?" He holds up his taser, the sapphire electrodes at the end of the stick cackling. I nod, having felt the wrath of those many times over the past week. "Wise decision. It's time to meet your maker, kid."

The Shadow Warden grabs my shoulder and hauls me off the floor and into the hallway outside. Shadow Wardens are one of the highest forms of guards in the magics world and anyone who values their life is frightened of them, for good reason. They literally use shadows to move around and have superhuman combat skills to boot. Every fiber of my being is telling me to shut up and not push my luck, but I've got to at least try...

"Why am I here? I don't know what happened. Please tell me?" I beg, just like I always do with the guards, but they couldn't look more disinterested if they tried. "I really don't know what's going on!"

"She's been saying that since we found her," the guard scoffs, pausing outside a set of towering wooden doors.

The Shadow Warden grunts at me. "Well, I'm sure this will jog her memory."

Wrapping his hand around the brass handle, he opens the doors and ushers me inside. The guard follows, his taser close to my back. Everything happens so quickly. I'm shoved into a glass box. More light penetrates my eyes, and I struggle to see or hear anything. My senses try to adjust to the light and fresh air I've been deprived of for what feels like an eternity. My legs tremble in their sockets, threatening to liquefy as I blink up at the lights. Slowly, my senses acclimate, and the blood drains from my face as I take stock of where I am. I know this courtroom all too well.

My mother often held hearings here and I was allowed to watch from the gallery. Now I'm up in the Box, facing the Grand Warden and his four High Wardens, but I don't know what crime I'm being tried for.

"Izora Dawn, do you swear on Selena to tell us the whole truth of the events of what we ask you?"

I blink up at the Grand Warden's sullen face. "Where... where am I?"

"Answer the question, Shadowborn," another voice demands.

I follow the voice to the shadows at my left, where the darkness seems to gather. There are no lights at that side of the bar. I think it's where the jury's sitting, but I'm not sure. I can barely breathe up here let alone think straight.

"Quiet," one of the other High Warden commands, the only female of the group. She casts a cold glance at the voice and then trains her eyes back on me. "Do you swear to tell the truth?"

My heart stammering in my chest, I choke out, "Yes, I swear. But please... I don't know what I did... where I am... what's going on..."

The Grand Warden waves his hand and light bleeds through the darkness concealing the rest of the room. The jury consists of two men and two women. Beside them are the Shadow Warden and the guard who brought me here. I spot my mother at the front of the gallery on the other side, her eyes bloodshot and face streaked with tears. My step-father is on her right, but he's not looking at me, and my step-sister glowers beside him. I feel dizzy and sick just looking at their faces. This can't really be happening, can it? It all feels too painful and surreal. Further up the gallery, my gaze lands on the men and women all dressed in white lab coats, just like...

Everything hits me in one ravening wave.

The injection on the back of my neck. The pain. The wings. The power.

The memories come flooding back and I collapse to

the floor, my fall cushioned by more white padding. Tears slide off my face and seep into the ground. Whatever those monsters did to me, I'm being punished for it. But I never asked for any of this. I never *wanted* to be abducted and tortured into a Light Fae. I search the courtroom in a daze, finding my mother again. But the pain I see in her eyes it too much, and I look away. Does she really believe that I'm innocent? Or does she think I'm guilty?

"Izora, you are charged with five accounts of murder," the Grand Warden resumes. "How do you plead?"

My answer is instantaneous.

"*Not* guilty! They took me from the academy and tortured me into becoming a light fae. I'm telling the truth!" My voice cracks and echoes around the courtroom. The only other noise is my mother as she sobs into a handkerchief. I can hardly look at her as she wipes her tears, pushing her silver hair behind her ears. A habit I've seen her do a million times when something is wrong. Usually, it's my evil step-sister who did something, not me.

I've never fucked up like this. I always follow the rules, just enough to get by and live a normal life.

There's whispering among the jury. The badges on their suit coats flash in the lights, and I realise some of them are junior wardens and others simply keepers.

"Lying to us will only make your case worse," the blond male High Warden at the end announces. "You were found in a wrecked building with the incinerated remains of five innocent Shadow Wardens. There is so much proof against you that I fear you will just lie no matter what we discuss here."

I gape at him, an immediate feeling of cold dread rushing into me. By his scathing expression alone, he's the kind of warden who won't listen even if I did have all the evidence stacked in my favour. I doubt any of the people here will listen. Five of their own kin—who kidnapped and tortured me—found dead with only me as a survivor? Of course it'll be easier for them to pin their deaths on me. That way they can cover up their dirty work.

I look over at my mother, barely holding back my tears. "Mum, you know I wouldn't do this! Please, help me?"

I plaster myself to the glass. My mother shadowlocates to the front of the box and places her shaking hands opposite mine, her grey eyes completely empty. And that terrifies me. My mother's eyes are always lit up even in her darkest moments.

More voices talk and throw accusations at me.

"I didn't kill them," I tell my mother, letting my tears fall but standing tall.

Looking into her eyes, she knows it's true.

I'm being set up.

"...then it is decided. We find you, Izora Dawn, guilty of high murder of the five wardens you so viciously killed for your own selfish gain," the Grand Warden announces. "The punishment will be four years in Shadowborn Prison. Upon completing your sentence, you shall be sent to live alone in the mortal world, wherein you will be an outcast and shunned from this world for the rest of your life. The Enchanted Forest will no longer be welcoming to you, nor will the people and creatures who live in it."

As the Grand Warden declares my sentence with a knock of his hammer, I can only stare at my mother as she slides down the glass and bursts into tears. She's whispering something over and over again that I can't quite make out at first, but when I finally do, I really wish I hadn't.

"I always knew you would end up here. I'm sorry... I'm sorry I could not stop them."

"Do you accept your four-year sentence to Shadowborn Prison to repent for your sins?" the Grand Warden concludes, but I can't bring myself to look at them, too distraught by the sight of my mother falling apart before me.

I scratch at the glass in an attempt to reach out and touch her, my own tears flowing silently down my cheeks. My step-father, without even looking at me, pulls her from the box and takes her away, leaving me alone, falsely accused and convicted of a crime I did not commit.

"Izora, do you accept your fate?" the Grand Warden repeats, his hammer ready to knock again.

"Yes," I finally answer as they drag me out of the room.

CHAPTER TWO

Izora

DYING IS A LUXURY IN THIS WORLD AND PEOPLE like me don't deserve it. At least, that's what I'm told by the Shadow Warden dragging me out of the carriage and into the grounds of Shadowborn Prison. No, sentencing me to death would've been far too easy. The Grand Warden wants me to suffer as my victims did.

My victims.

A hollow numbness racks through me as I follow the warden through the wrought-iron gates. The prison building is even more terrifying than the rumours. I guess it would have to be since the words etched into the gates are 'only the dangerous thrive'. Really sets the tone for the next four years of my life here, doesn't it? I'm sure many who stand in front of this prison feel guilt, regret, or possibly like me, the need to escape before they've even stepped foot over the threshold. It's a horrible, gut-wrenching feeling. But it's also my life now.

The prison is one large concrete building with towering electric fences and stone towers on each corner. Bright beams shine and move around the prison, illuminating every tiny crevice, cementing the fact that there's no place to hide. Not even the shadows are safe anymore. The building looks like a castle straight out of a horror movie, complete with a cemetery at the front entrance. Everywhere I look, I see guards walking around with tasers and guns, and I have no doubt they are well-trained wardens, if not Shadow Wardens themselves.

Only the dangerous survive Shadowborn Prison. The rest are nothing but stones to stand on.

My mother's words come back to haunt me, and a chill sweeps through my body. I look up at the highest point of the prison, where the tip of the spire gleams against the crescent moon nestled in the twilight sky. It looks almost beautiful and that wasn't what I was expecting. Beauty hidden in dangerous lies.

"Hurry up, sweetheart!"

The Shadow Warden pokes me in the ribs again with his taser. Despite my best efforts not to show any signs of weakness, I hunch over and let out a sharp hiss, tears stinging my eyes from the electric shock.

I want to shove that stick up his arse and see how he likes it.

I actually contemplate doing just that, but I wisely convince myself otherwise. While pissing the guards off on day one is tempting, it's not a smart move and I need to be smart to stay alive. I have no idea what or whom I'm up against here, and one thing my messed-up family taught me is to be strong no matter what. I'm innocent and the only way I'm going to prove that is by doing my time here and then getting out so I can find out what *really* happened to me, why my dark magic isn't working anymore and why I remember being turned into a light fae. Until my time is up, I need to play it safe if I want to make it out alive.

Lifting my head and ignoring the hands that cruelly seize my arms, I step into the prison, leaving my pride and freedom at the door. I guess I won't need them here. I have a funny feeling my self-defense lessons and combat training at Shadowborn Academy will come in useful. I may look like a tiny girl who slightly resembles Tinkerbell, but by Selena I can fight when need be.

I'm pushed through security and strip-searched for the second time today. I try to forget every single second of it, digging these memories into the back of my mind so I only have to relive them in my nightmares. My handcuffs are unlocked, and I sigh a breath of relief which one of the keepers merely laughs at.

"Smile, Izora. You aren't as pretty when you frown."

The Shadow Warden's comment only makes me want to attack him, to show him I'm not just a pretty face that he can bully. I push down that urge, knowing it's not going to do me any good.

A female keeper steps forward, holding a heavy metal collar that glows sapphire like the tips of the tasers, with a bold number engraved on the front. 4399. I know straight away that this inmate number is now my only identity here. I fear the collar before she even presses it to my neck and activates the magic. I've heard shadowborns talking about this like it's a joke and parents threatening to use them on their misbehaving children. Magic collars serve only one purpose: to suck the powers out from shadowborns' souls when they dare to use them, and from what I remember my mother telling me, to feed the magical walls of this prison.

Once I'm stripped of my clothing, the wardens and keepers talk amongst themselves as if I'm not even here. I pull my thick, silver hair out of the collar, letting the wavy strands fall to my waist and cover me up a little. I've never once cared about nudity, but this is different. I can feel their eyes on me, and I can't escape them.

I'm not in control anymore.

How can I go from being a damn good student at Shadowborn Academy to the new arrival at Shadowborn Prison in the space of a week?

They take me into another room, and a rush of cold dread fills me when I spot the showers lined up against the tiled wall. Thankfully, only two female wardens come into the room with me, not that it makes this process any easier as I can guess the next step. Tears sting my eyes from the sheer indignation of it all, standing here naked, collared like some beast.

Ice-cold water sprays over my body as the female hoses me down. I gasp at the coldness and try to hide my body from them but it's pointless. I eventually give in, lowering my arms and letting them wash away my tears with the water. Once they are done, the wardens dump a pile of plain black clothes into my soaking wet arms.

"You've got two minutes to get dressed before the next lot arrive."

With that, they leave me in the silence of the shower room. I'm thankful for the limited time alone. My mother always said it's horrible to be on your own, that we are destined to be around other shadowborns and fae. Social creatures and all that bullshit. I always told her that being alone is the only time I feel safe… and safety is something rare in this world.

I stand there for a moment in complete shock, shivering and cold, before pulling on the clothes. They smell like lavender but they feel cheap and rough against my ivory skin. The bra and panties are a size too big, but they'll do. The socks feel good against my feet until I wobble a little and put my foot down in the water, getting my sock wet. Grumbling, I pull the black combat boots on and hug myself. I rub my arms, fruitlessly trying to put some heat back into my numb body. The tears I've been suppressing threaten to roll down my cheeks, but I bite my lip, refusing to let them fall. Now isn't the time for tears. Now is the time for survival, and soon enough, revenge. I've just got to get through my first day.

Outside the room, the female who hosed me down is whispering into someone else's ear.

Warden Luke. He is handsome, alluringly so with his glacier-blue eyes and copper hair that curls at the ends. Topped with his sexy as hell body, he's every girl's dream. Many at Shadowborn Academy followed him around like lost puppies, desperate for any little bit of attention he would throw their way. The only issue with Warden Luke? He's an asshole like most of the wardens in this world. Wardens are stuck-up guards with shit loads of power to protect the Enchanted Forest and everything in it. I don't think I've ever met a warden who didn't think Shadowborns were below them and useful for nothing more than pawns in their game. It's true that Shadowborns are the lowest of the magical society, with fae being at the top, but you know what they say about an underdog?

We come out fighting.

I used to really like this guy, at least when he worked at the academy and happily came to our parties. Then he got promoted and I knew he was transferred here. Now he's a typical Shadow Warden, all pretty boy looks and light magic that makes him feel superior to Shadowborns like me. I can see it in his gaze, the smugness, the 'I'm better than you' look. His dark eyes never leave my own as he steps forward with his taser at the ready. At least the other Shadow Warden is gone.

"You'll meet your induction officer soon. Until then, I'll go over the basics and show you to your cell." Luke walks over to the door at the other end of the room, and my blood runs cold in my veins but I'm too exhausted to put up a fight.

In all honesty, I just want to curl up into a ball and die.

It's not like there is much in my life to go back home to now. I'm not even allowed to see my family or friends after I've served my sentence. Every part of my life I planned out is now impossible. I don't know who I'm meant to be at this point.

"Don't I get to call my family?" I ask quietly, looking between him and the female keeper. It's a long shot but it's worth it. However, their silence speaks volumes, and a nervous lurch cleaves through my stomach. There's nothing I can do but follow him into the dimly lit hallway.

Everything is suffocatingly quiet. The steel doors lining the grey-pitted walls are an imposing sight, each of them containing a vertical slot where I suspect food trays and other items are slid through. The cells must be soundproof, too, because I can't hear a thing from the other side. You'd think the lack of screaming would put me at ease. It doesn't. It makes this place feel more like a morgue than a prison block. Gods, it gives me the creeps. I already can't wait to see the back of it.

"You'll find Shadowborn Prison harsh but fair," the warden informs me, not bothering to glance back as he leads the way. "Follow the rules set in place and you'll survive just fine. Break them and you'll be placed in solitary confinement until the governor deems otherwise. Further black marks against your name and, well, you'll find out just how harsh this prison can really be. Understand, jaybird?"

I nod, swallowing the lump in my throat. "Who is the governor, Shadow Warden?"

"You'll meet him soon enough. If you want to survive here, follow the Governor's rules. Lockdown is from six p.m. until eight a.m., and your ass stays in its cell within those hours. Outside of them, you're free to roam wherever you want so long as you remain on prison grounds."

That surprises me a little. I guess I thought they'd be keeping us cooped up in our cells all the time.

Luke swipes his access card down the reader on a set of electric doors. They peel to the side, unveiling a spacious grey room with an enormous steel cage in the middle of the white padded floor. There's nothing inside the cage apart from a small single bed, a steel toilet and a sink. Talk about bare necessities. It takes me a moment to realise that this cell—this *cage*—is meant for me.

"A cage?" I glance between the cage and the warden. "Why? I'm not exactly a threat to anyone."

The edge of the warden's lips twitch. "Who said you were the threat?"

My heart sinks into the pit of my stomach, but before I can say anything, he's removing my handcuffs and shoving me into the cage. My feet sink into the padded floor and my heart lurches into my throat. It's worse than the glass dock back in the courtroom. And this is my home now. My life. My punishment for a crime I was forced to commit in self-defense.

"There's an emergency call button in there should you need it," Luke says, pointing to the red button on the other side of the gate's metal lock. "Just don't waste my time, you hear? I'm not your goddamn therapist. I don't give a fuck about how you feel or what shit's keeping you up at night. My job is to make sure you stay alive and follow the rules of this prison. A daughter of a High Warden, who put most people in here, isn't going to be unnoticed."

He slams the gate, and the steel bars hum around me, activated by whatever magic binds me here. I watch him walk away. Without even a backward glance, he says, "You're in here for your own protection. Endure and die here, jaybird, or fight and thrive. It's entirely up to you."

I sink to my knees and push my back against the iron bars, pressing my fingers into the cushioned floor. Tears of rage quickly replace the tears from before. Rage at being convicted of a crime I never even committed. Rage at the injustice. Rage at the fact that they think I'm going to accept my fate here without putting up a fight.

I'm from the House of Dawn.

We do not surrender easily.

CHAPTER THREE

Izora

WHEN LUKE TURNS ON THE LIGHT AND bangs at my gate, an urge to throttle the handsome warden consumes me. I barely got a wink of sleep last night, and after finally drifting off for what feels like only seconds, here's my own personal demon arrived to make my life hell all over again.

I lie on my back, my eyes closed against the cruelty of the blinding light in here. It's funny how I miss sunlight bursting through the windows to my room at Shadowborn Academy and how my roommate used to snore. I even miss the bedsheets which always smelt like magic and cotton. This bed smells like stale soda. In those few moments after waking up, I almost forget where I am or what happened yesterday. It's like when you're awake but not quite, still lost in your dream while the real world ceases to exist. But just like with my dreams, the illusion quickly slips through my fingers, and reality dawns on me.

I'm not home or at Shadowborn Academy.

I shoot my eyes open, my pulse spiking as the panic kicks in and fills every vessel in my body. The metallic glare of the ceiling bars gleams down, confirming that this wasn't an illusion. I really am imprisoned here, caged like a bird whose wings aren't broken, just her spirit.

"Time for breakfast in Hell, jaybird."

My stomach recoils at the thought of eating. "Shockingly, I don't have much of an appetite. I think I'll pass."

The warden huffs under his breath. "They all say that. The food here ain't nothin' to write home about, but after what you'll see today, you'll be glad you ate somethin'. Not many bring themselves to eat for a few days afterwards."

I sit up in bed and scowl at him. "You're so comforting, you know that, warden?"

He slides his taser along the bars of my cage, the rattling sound like nails on a chalkboard. "Get movin.'"

I watch him leave, glaring at the back of his skull in an attempt to throw literal daggers at him. But nothing happens. There's just an empty feeling in my gut that reminds me of the collar binding my magic. I understand why they force us to wear them. The governor had to do something to control the powerful inmates of his supernatural prison. I just can't shake the gaping hole in the pit of my stomach. It's like a hunger I'll never be able to satiate without my magic.

By all accounts, I should be glad that I can no longer use magic after the 'accidents' I caused in my youth. That's what my mother called killing my nanny and burning various buildings down to the ground, including our summer house in Helios—all accidents.

Funny alternative for the words murder and arson.

To this day, I'm still haunted by Emma's screams as she burned alive and how I could do nothing but cry and scream for someone to help her. I turned into a shadowborn when I drowned in the river near the burning summer house as my stupid seven-year-old ass thought I could swim to the other side of the lake to get help. Since the river connected to the Faerie Pools, where all magic in our world begins, my body adapted in the only way it could to save my life.

The magic pulsing through my dying little body *darkened*.

I became known as a shadowborn—dark magic users that are considered the dregs of society. My mother never wanted to admit this, so she turned a blind eye to my shifting abilities. Goddess forbid the rest of the Enchanted Forest found out a Grand Warden's child had become a shadowborn and not a pure-blooded light magic like I should have been. No, my mother thought that by hiding me, nobody would catch on and we could live a normal life.

That didn't work for long.

My shadowborn magic loved to burn things down too much. By the time I was twelve, it was even more out of control and could not be hidden. First, it was little things like a tree by our houses. Then it got worse, endangering the lives of more people. Eventually, my mother had to admit that it was me who burnt the summer house down and got into the lake, dying and becoming a shadowborn. Apparently, it was a massive scandal at the time. But I wouldn't know, I wasn't allowed to leave the house. This was also the time she met my step-father and step-sister and thought a new family would help ground me.

It did the complete opposite.

Am I the least bit thankful that my mother lied for me, all these years later?

I glance around the cage, soaking up the confines of my newest prison.

Not really.

Sighing, I push off my bed and look around for the clothes I dumped on the floor some hours ago. I'm surprised to find them folded next to a large plastic bag by the gate. When the hell did someone come into my cage? I rummage through it and drag out clothes that definitely do not belong to me; white and grey tank tops, tee-shirts, sweatpants, a pair of black jeans, socks, and panties, followed by some meager bathroom necessities that include a hair brush and floss. I wonder if I can strangle myself with the latter.

Pushing that thought from my mind, I grab fresh underwear, a grey tank, jeans, and start to dress. I'm just pulling on my own tattered leather boots when Warden Luke opens the door.

"Time to go," he says, swiping his pass against the gate. They buzz open and he steps inside, his eyes locking with mine. We are both silent for a second, then he tilts his head to the side. "I remember you from the academy. You used to sneak in with Willow to our parties, right? Thought you looked familiar."

I throw my braid over my shoulder, scrunching my face up at him. "It's a bit creepy that you remember me, don't you think?"

His expression turns cold and I regret my words straight away. Dammit, I need to make friends and turn my resting bitch face off, as well as my sharp words. "Watch it, jaybird. I'm the only one in this joint who's gonna be protectin' your sorry ass, so don't go pissin' me off. Move."

He steps aside and motions to the door with his dimpled chin. I hate that he's right and that I do, in a lot of ways, depend on him to keep me safe. I've never felt this vulnerable before. Maybe having a sexy warden on my side isn't such a bad idea?

"Okay, okay." I lift my hands in supplication and slide past him into the hallway. "You're cute so I'll listen."

A flicker of a smile plays on his lips. "Get goin', Dawn."

I grin back at him and slowly veer down the hallway. Survival is a strong suit of mine, yet it's got nothing on my level of seduction. If I'm being framed for murder and trapped here against my will, I need to start making allies stat. It's time for Operation Unicorn—make friends in prison—and I figure Warden Luke is a good place to start.

He leads me into a corridor filled with female inmates who each give me an assessing glance. I keep my gaze fixed on the steel doors at the end, refusing to appear meek or timid despite being the freshest meat in the pack. I do notice one thing, though—their cells are all different from mine. They're actual prison cells instead of cages. Great. So I'm the only one who needs protection, as Luke put it. That could either make me look bad-ass or weak in this place. I need to make sure no one mistakes me for the latter, or I'll become the punching bag here.

At the end of the hallway, voices carry from the opposite the electric doors. My heart speeds up as I take a sharp breath.

Time to see what I'm up against.

Luke steers me into the mess hall crammed with inmates of both genders, all of them wearing the same collar as me. Most are sitting at the long tables with little plastic stools, eating food from trays or playing card games and trading items. At least twenty wardens guard the walls, keeping a close eye on their prisoners, and there's constant noise in the background; inmates chatting, doors buzzing, gates slamming, the electric click of the tasers and collars activating, wardens yelling commands, arguments and fights breaking out, voices sounding from the speakers at each corner of the hall.

The focal point is the servery at the other end where many are still gathered like vultures around a corpse. My stomach recoils at the thought of eating, but Luke may be right. Who knows how I'll feel after today is over? Maybe it's better to fill my stomach with something.

He guides me past the pool tables where all the men playing stop to look at me. It's like I've got five heads or something. I approach the servery by myself and grab some fruit.

"Hey, cutie. What you after?"

I pause at the front of the queue and look up at the inmate serving hot food. He winks at me and smiles, the soft dimples in his cheeks unexpectedly endearing. It seems to be the only thing soft about him—the rest of him is built like a bodybuilder. He's all muscle, with bulging tattooed arms and short dark hair. His eyes are the most striking though, like the blue of a flame, burning into my core.

There's a flutter threatening to kick off in my stomach, but I crush it down. Now isn't the time for getting all gooey-eyed over hot-as-fuck inmates. Now is the time for allies and survival, then later revenge.

"All right, Axel?" Luke greets him, folding his arms as he comes to a halt at my side.

"Is this your new cutie?" Axel asks the warden, shooting me another cheeky wink.

The muscles work hard around Luke's jaw. "Prisoner. I thought you were workin' in the arena now?"

"You know me, warden. I like to shake things up every now and then. Figured I'd also help out in the kitchen for a while."

As I watch their exchange, I slide a banana onto my

tray. The continental selection looks way more appetising than their fried stacks of heart attacks.

My stomach grumbling, I peel and take a bite of the banana. That's when I can't help but feel all the eyes burning into the side of my head. I glance at the men standing in the queue, impatiently waiting for Luke to shut up and go away. Sure enough, they're all staring like they've never seen a girl eat a banana before.

I look away and continue eating. It's hard not to lash out at them for their creepy leering, but I'm not in the 'normal' world anymore. I'm in a prison filled with goddess knows what.

Pick your battles.

"You ready, Dawn?"

I nod at Luke and prepare to walk away, but Axel's voice catches me.

"Dawn?" he repeats, lifting a middle finger to the guy who's bickering about waiting too long. "That's a pretty name."

"It's Izora," I tell him over my shoulder, throwing a smile at the last second. "Izora Dawn."

He grins at me and continues serving the others. Meanwhile, I follow Luke over to the bench by the barred window. A few girls already sitting there leave the second I sit down with my tray. At first, I think it's because of me, but as I look around the mess hall, I notice how none of the other inmates are being accompanied by their warden. There's many of them standing guard close by, but none are sitting with their wards. Only me.

"Watch out for Axel," Luke warns, leaning against the bench, his gaze fixed on the servery.

"He seemed all right," I counter quietly, finishing the last of my banana and tossing the skin onto my tray. "And I need to make friends here."

"I think you're forgetting somethin', jaybird. You're not at the academy anymore. You're in prison. Trust no one."

"Not even you?"

He looks my way then, and there's a strange glint in his cobalt eyes. "Not even me. Every person in this place would sooner slit your throat than help you out. Just wait until this afternoon. You'll see. The best thing to do is to keep your head down and stay away from people like Axel."

I force down another bit of fruit, though the grape seems to lodge in my throat. "Who is he?"

"He runs with Memphis's lot. The two of them pretty much rule the roost here, though some of the wardens beg to differ. Just be careful. There's only so much I can protect you from."

"Do you really care if I get hurt?" I press him, watching his reaction closely. "Or are you just worried about my pretty face?"

Luke arches a brow and looks away, shaking his head. I think he's about to laugh, but then he pushes off the bench and his expression sours. "Eat up, it's time to go."

CHAPTER FOUR

Izora

I stuff what fruit I can into my mouth and follow him out of the mess hall. Now that I've realised I'm the only one with a different cell and a Shadow Warden bodyguard, I understand why everyone's eyes are drawn to me. I really do stick out like a sore thumb.

This is my mother's fault and I know I'm going to get punished for her life choices. Being a Grand Warden is everything to her and she told me once that her record for proving cases as guilty was unbeaten. For all I know, she could've sentenced everyone in here. I can't really blame the inmates for hating me. It's just going to make my idea of Operation Unicorn all the harder. I thought about it all night and even gave my master plan a name. You know, to make it real and all. Operation Unicorn is my plan to get close to the governor, somehow, and then get my ass out of here.

It's not a great and well thought out plan...yet.

Luke escorts me through the maze of hallways as my thoughts scramble. The sunlight darkens the deeper we venture into the bowels of the prison. I follow him up three flights of seemingly never-ending stairs. Wherever he's taking me, the other inmates are also gathering there. They happily run past me on the stairs, and their excited chatter fills my ears.

After the fourth staircase, we join a crowd of people gathered inside an auditorium. There's nothing inside apart from TV screens and benches. It makes the hall cold and carries voices around like an echo. The main wall at the back consists of crystal-clear glass, but I can see the corners of the windows shimmering in the light, signalling it's a magical structure. That's not what seems to have captured everyone's attention. It's the gorge inside and the pile of dead bodies that lay there.

"Yikes. This week is a total bloodbath," an inmate states beside me.

I flinch at her words, listening closely.

"Well, it is in the name, genius," her friend remarks. "They don't call it the Blood Trials for nothing. Told you Tom would die. Pay up, you owe me."

Her friend grumbles and hands over a packet of cigarettes. "I should've known he wouldn't stand a chance against that Alpha. Markle is a nasty sort."

Bile rises into my throat. Were those girls betting on whose dead body they'd find? I glance anxiously at Luke, who's also staring out the window, and then back at the gorge. Inmates in pale blue scrubs fish out the bodies with machinery to dump them on the surface, which is the same level as us. The gorge itself is more like an arena carved into the ground, but it stretches so far down that I can't see the surface.

A man in a sharp mahogany suit steps out of the window and the glass ripples like water. Some applaud his arrival, mostly wardens and keepers, and the hall falls eerily silent as he takes centre stage.

"Another successful event," he begins in a deep, powerful voice. "For those eager to sign up to next week's Blood Trials, you may do so now, but I caution you to bring more than strength to the table. Only the strongest make it out of this arena alive." Glancing at the few sniffling in the audience, his dragon-like eyes flash like molten gold as he adds indifferently, "The Green Room is available to those who seek counselling. You may pay tribute to the deceased once what remains of their bodies has been identified."

I gawp at the man, digesting his every word and syllable. He's obviously the governor. I feel sick just from listening to him, but every single person in here, including the guards, hang on to his words like it's gospel. He's a little more rugged than I expected from a governor. His ash brown hair is short and shaved at the sides but locks fall onto his forehead, accentuating the symbols tattooed on the side of his face. He's beautiful, yet it's a deadly kind of beauty, like a ruse I bet he uses to lure unsuspecting victims into his traps. Beautiful and wild. His golden, reptilian eyes are almost hypnotic. The only other person I've seen with eyes like this is Zander, the Shadow Warden back at the academy, and I know it means they're descended from Draconians. Figures they'd put a Draconian in charge of the prison. They're the harshest species in the entire Forest.

"I'd like to welcome all of our newest inmates," the governor resumes. "I trust your induction this week will go smoothly. I'm the governor. You can call me Gov or Gold, whatever the fuck floats your boat..." He pauses and a dark shadow drifts over his face. "My rules here are simple enough. Follow them, you and I will get on just fine. Break them, and it might be the last thing you ever do. Now, as for the Blood Trials. You enter at your own risk, and once you sign up, there is no way out unless you beat me in the final round. I've seen most of you fight and I know why you're here, but trust me, you won't win. Other than in the training rooms and arena, we don't hurt inmates. You have a problem? Tell a warden and I will sort it if I think it's worth my time."

"I think I can take you," some fool shouts.

Gold merely affords him a dry laugh. "Then sign up. Prove your worth to me. The Blood Trials' prizes are worth it. You will win a better room, with your own tv, a double bed and all the luxuries of the human world."

"I will!" The same idiot who spoke all but sneers. "And then we will see who is boss then."

With a smile, Gold walks right up to the now nervous prisoner and looks down at him like he's filthy. "When you piss yourself in the arena and beg for your pitiful life, I'm going to laugh and let you die a long, painful death. Congratulations on catching my attention."

A chill slides down the length of my spine. How can someone so beautiful be this inhumane? He's talking about it all like we're just meat—as if this 'Blood Trials' is simply a sport he enjoys to watch and participate in.

Too busy watching his exchange with the prisoner, I don't notice the girls moving from my side. I do, however, notice the hard pinch of my ass, and I spin around, glaring up into the face of a class A jerk.

"Nice and firm, babe. Just what I like."

White-hot fury bubbles through me.

"Leave the fresh meat alone," another guy tells him, pulling on his shoulder.

I clench my hands into tight fists. I know I shouldn't do this. I know I should be making allies here, not enemies. But there's one thing I cannot stand for—people who think it's perfectly okay to sexually assault others. I couldn't give a flying fuck if this guy is an expert predator. I'm not letting it side.

Before Luke can restrain me, I muster all my strength, all the anger and hurt I've been bottling up since I was sentenced, and I release it by punching this ass right in the fucking throat.

The idiot wasn't expecting it.

He falls down like a sack of bricks and lands on the floor with a thud that everyone makes room for. My hand throbs as if I've broken it, but it's a good kind of pain.

Guards rush over, including Luke, and they seize me, but then the governor lifts his hand, just barely, and they all stop. Their tasers and guns fall by their side, and they step away from me. When I look back at the governor's face, I find that he's smirking, almost like he's impressed by what I just did.

"Let that be a reminder to those who break my rules." His incineration eyes search the crowd coldly, and the smile falls from his face like melted snow. "As I just stated a few moments ago for all you dumbasses, under no circumstances are you allowed to lay a hand on another inmate. If you want to act like an animal, you save it for in the Blood Trials. Beyond those walls, you keep your hands to fucking yourself or I'll have every last bone in your body pounded into dust." Clearing his throat, he resumes as if nothing happened. "Now, where the fuck was I..."

My jaw hangs open, stunned by his reaction. I expected to be punished for retaliating—not pretty much congratulated. Luke digs his fingers into my shoulder and spins me around towards the exit.

"You're right," I whisper to him, my body shaking with adrenaline as he drags me away. "This is Hell."

CHAPTER FIVE

Izora

LUKE DOESN'T SAY A WORD AS PUSHES ME DOWN THE many flights of stairs. His light magic literally cackles from him in anger, even lifting the hairs on my own body. By that alone, I can tell he's a powerful Shadow Warden.

A powerful and pissed off one.

"Where are you taking me now?" I dare to ask him over my shoulder. "I'm sorry I lashed out back there. That guy was a fucking creep and I couldn't just put up with it. Then everyone would think I'm an easy target."

Luke stops short and glares at me. "I get that. What you really need to get into your head is that you're locked up with people worse than him. You're just gonna make my job harder if you go keep goin' around tryna assert your stupid dominance."

I frown at him, irked by the words. "I'm not just some silly little girl."

His features soften a little. Damn if it doesn't do something to me. "You can handle yourself, I'll give you that. That punch wasn't half bad. But choose your battles wisely, or I'm gonna have nothin' but blood to clean up once you're gone. Give me your hands."

I hold out my hands, deciding not to push him further. Operation Unicorn really depends on me getting on his good side.

Luke handcuffs me again and my frown returns. Then again, maybe this means he's taking me outside? It'd be nice to get some fresh air.

He continues leading me back to the front of the prison. Instead of entering the girl's wing, he takes me out of the main rooms. I still can't shake the images of the dead bodies from my mind. The way the inmates just hauled them out like they were nothing… Is this really my life now? Is this really all I'm worth—people making bets over?

Not if I can do anything about it. I'm not going to be one of those bodies lying at the pit of the arena. If need be, I'll use their bodies as a ladder to get out.

On the other side of the hallway, a pair of wardens take their sweet-ass time opening the gate, then we step through it. Luke pauses outside a row of doors with frosted glass windows. Every single one of them is guarded by two wardens who barely blink our way.

Luke turns to the wardens with an annoyed frown. "Room three is activated."

In seconds, the doors siphon open and Luke pulls me

into the third room. I barely step over the threshold before he stalks back out, shutting the door behind him. I look around the room where there is one chair facing a pool of shimming white water. It looks almost like milk from way back here. Not having a clue what this place is, I sit down on the chair and stare into the pool. The surface bubbles like it's simmering and a sphere of water floats into the air. It slowly blurs and transforms into the image of my mother in her office back home. Her normally cold eyes are bloodshot, the bags under them heavy and blue, and the exhaustion on her face is evident. She must have just got back from work because she still has her court robes on and her blonde hair is slicked back into a tight bun, so tight it pulls her skin back.

My lips part in surprise. The image is so clear it's like she's in the same room with me. I've never communicated this way before and I can hardly believe what I'm seeing. I figure this must be magical water sourced from the Faerie Pools, but I didn't know you could do this with it.

"Mum?"

She wipes her eyes with a handkerchief and gives a pained half-smile. "Izora, my darling child. How did this ever happen to us?" Her voice cracks ever so slightly, which is unlike her. We're both obviously aware that this phone call of sorts is being recorded. She's always told me that one can never appear weak in our world, or in any world, now I think about it. So why is she letting herself cry like this? I don't think I've ever seen her shed a tear in my eighteen years.

Clearing my throat, I squirm on my chair, at a loss for words. I've wanted to see her so badly but now I'm here, I only feel lost and scared.

And clueless.

Thankfully, my mother speaks first and I'm not left looking like a lost lamb.

"How are they treating you?"

"Fine," I dryly answer and her face falls for a moment before she gets her composure back. Was she expecting me to rave about the five-start treatment? "How are you? How's Ez and Willow?"

Another sniffle, and it actually makes me choke up a little. "We are all still in shock. Your step-father cannot believe what happened. Willow has come back from the Shadowborn Academy to spend time grieving your loss at home with her family."

I have to bite my tongue from calling bullshit on that last part. Willow never did want me as a sister and she made damn sure I knew that from the start. The only reason Willow is faking some sisterly love now is because she wants something. I doubt even my step-father is at all affected by this.

"Are you going to plead my case?" I ask my mother, rubbing my hands together as another chill sweeps over me. "You know I would never lie to you, Mum. Whoever those wardens were, they kidnapped me and turned me into a light fae. I had wings and everything, and even though they're gone now, I know the whole thing was real."

She sighs, crossing her arms and watching me with pity-filled eyes. "I know this isn't what you want to hear, darling, and I'm sure you didn't mean to kill those wardens, but your story doesn't add up. I've tried everything in my power to get evidence to back up your word. So far, there is none."

Frustrated by her response, I can only nod.

This is the woman I know. Cold, stern, and straight to the point. No beating around the bush.

"Izora, you never once asked about your father growing up," she adds, her tone a little softer. "But I want you to know that he was brave. Many admired him for his courage."

Tears prick my eyes at the mention of my dead father. "I once found your old journal and I read about my father. The only thing that stuck with me all these years later was the saying you wrote about. 'The House of Dawn never surrenders', and I don't want to know more."

A wan smile pulls at her lips. "Your father never gave up. I can tell you more than that journal ever could. You only need to ask."

I'm surprised by the beseeching edge to her voice. My father died before I was born. He was a normal Shadow Warden for the light fae. There isn't anything else to know about who I am with regards to my father. I read that he was a good fighter, though he liked to play dirty, and he was well-respected. He met my mother at a ball in Helios and they fell in love right away. It was all very romantic. Then he died protecting King Ulric, the Light

Fae King, from an attack when my mother was nine months pregnant with me, just days away from birth.

"Does it matter now that he is dead?" I ask, tilting my head at her. "I think the made-up ideas of a father in my mind are safer than what you could tell me."

"Izora, listen to me—" she cuts off, and the room plunges into darkness.

Alarms blast in the background behind me, yet my mother still speaks, her voice much more urgent now.

"Stay alive, Izora! You are telling the truth and my daughter will not be locked up for long. I will find the evidence. Stay alive and keep your head down. I know I never say it but I do love you, my darling baby girl!"

The lights blast back on as the alarms stop and the sphere drops into the water, splashing my legs as my heart pounds in my chest. Luke barrels into the room as I stand up and turn around, his eyes searching for some kind of danger I suspect.

"Did your mother say anything when the lights were out? We couldn't hear on the speakers," he demands, his cheek popping once.

It makes me wonder if my mother had anything to do with the blackout. And if so, *how?*

"Nothing," I say, shrugging. "The sphere just dropped into the water."

"Come on, we better get you back." He grabs my arm and turns for the door.

I don't know why, but I reach out and let my hand fall on his arm.

"Thanks for letting me have a phone call of sorts," I whisper, giving a genuine smile.

For a moment, he just looks at my hand, and then he nods. "It's nothing." His hand returning to my arm, he lowers his voice. "But don't tell the others. Inmates aren't allowed calls in the first month and after that, they have to earn them."

I keep silent as we go through the gates again and past the guards. A million thoughts run through my mind. I'm touched by his gesture, but now I owe him. Perhaps that doesn't need to be a bad thing.

I search his cold expression from the side as we walk down the corridor. "Why would you do that for me?"

He shrugs. "I guess I wanted to see you smile."

His answer does make me smile and feel in danger at the same time.

I have a feeling this Shadow Warden has a few secrets up his sleeve. I just hope they don't come to bite me in the ass one of these days.

CHAPTER SIX

Izora

THE NEXT MORNING, LUKE ACCOMPANIES ME TO the mess hall again. I'm relieved when he decides to speak to one of his colleagues instead of shadowing my every movement. He doesn't stray far, but I manage to reach the servery on my own. I'm a little bummed to see Axel isn't around.

"What's on the menu today then?" I muse, more to myself as I gather some food onto my tray. I feel a little guilty as I look for a table to sit down and eat. Luke said not many are able to eat once they see all the dead bodies getting fished out of the arena, but after talking to my mother, I find myself determined not to surrender. I may not have known my father, but one thing I do have is his courage and my mother's cunning.

My eyes trace the hall for the governor. He doesn't seem to be here, or if he is, I can't see him. I do notice something odd though. Right above the entrance hangs four glass cages. They look like the one I'm housed in except the entire front wall is made of glass that looks into the hall. Only one of them is occupied, and the female inmate is slouched against the glass so nobody can see her eating. I have a feeling those aren't maximum security cages. More like solitary confinement.

I pass by a table and catch part of a group's conversation.

"I wonder who the next poor fool is they have coming here to teach us?"

The guy next to him laughs. "Considering the last teacher fucked half the prison, anyone new is going to be a disappointment if they don't do the same. She was the best damn teacher I had."

I sit at the next table and stare at the pitiful excuse for porridge, the soggy looking bread and a carton of milk. I stir the clumpy porridge and barely manage to eat half when two women sit down opposite me.

"Where did you learn to hit like that?" the one with spiky blue hair and black, dagger-like eyes asks me.

She's a little stout, almost like she steals a lot of the food here. My point is proven when she takes my toast off my plate and starts munching away. Lucky for her, I don't care. Her blue hair makes me think of a friend of mine back at the academy and damn I miss Corvina Charles' snarky nature. I miss my friends and how they could make me feel safe. It was like I had a family when I was with them.

The blonde next to her rolls her eyes. "Clearly it was just a good shot. Anyway, I'm Janis Roth and this is my sister, Sharon. We part of the Blood Trials committee and wondered if you want to sign up."

My blood runs cold at the thought.

"No thanks," I reply with a tight smile. "I don't want to die for nice shit in here. As the humans say, you can't put a flower in an asshole and call it a vase."

Sharon bursts into laughter but it sounds fake to my ears. "Good one, jailbait."

I eye her cautiously before standing from the table and leaving. I have absolutely no intention of killing myself for a fancy room. I walk over to the bin and throw the rest of my food away, my appetite suddenly gone.

Figuring it's best that I head back to my cage, I leave the mess hall through the other exit at the front. I pause when I find a sign that says 'TRAINING' and my ears pick up the sound of heavy grunts and punches. I head through the double doors and into a guarded area where dozens of inmates are training in a gym-style setting. But it's no ordinary gym. The equipment is high-tech with holographic dummies that explode into stars when they're defeated by an inmate.

I spot Luke with a group of wardens and several others walking around, always watching. He must've come here while those girls tried to coax me into an early grave.

Yeah, as if I'll ever be signing up for the Blood Trials, girls.

I'd rather slit my own throat than have someone else

do it. Dead centre of the room is a chair shaped like a throne, and lo and behold, sitting in it is no other than Governor Gold. His eyes watch his subjects like the scum he thinks we all are. It riles my blood.

Feeling a shadow hang over me, I look up to see a giant of a man at my side.

"Watching him is gunning for trouble, kid."

"Maybe I like trouble," I counter, but my reply only makes him laugh, a bellowing sound that can't help but smile at.

Whoever this dude is, I figure he could crush ten people in his hands and not even feel a muscle pop. He must be at least seven feet, his enormous, muscular body covered in tiny scars and tattoos. He has a vest shirt hanging off his muscular chest, and tight trousers topped with heavy boots that could crush a man's skull in seconds. I would guess he is in his late thirties, maybe older going by his slightly greying, short blond hair, and he doesn't look at me like I'm a piece of meat as I've seen most the idiots in here do.

Most girls would shit their pants at the sight of a guy like him.

And there must be something wrong with me because I'm intrigued about why he's talking to me.

"Tell you what, kid, between your smart mouth and mean right hook, I might have found my new best friend. No one would ever suspect you talk like that and punch hard enough to take a man down. Who taught you?"

I cross my arms, twitching my nose. "Mostly

self-taught, to be honest. The Shadowborn Academy helped me perfect my skills though. I was the only student in my class that bothered to learn self-defense outside of using magic to defend themselves."

He thinks about my words for a moment. "Why did you?"

"I don't ever want to be weak and my powers could always be taken, so I had to have a backup plan. Looks like it worked out in the end."

His big hand falls on my shoulder, and I meet his grey eyes. "I'm Memphis Hasting, and don't worry, you can trust me. I don't expect you to listen. In fact, I would be disappointed if you did right away, but yeah, I'm here and first warning of our new friendship. Don't attract Gold's attention. You won't survive him. Two: Next time you knock a guy out, hit him in the balls. If he wakes up, he won't be able to chase you."

I can't help but snort at the last bit. "Sound advice."

I repeat his name in my head so I don't forget it. Memphis? More like Fuckphis. You could climb this guy like a tree. And then his name suddenly hits me. Luke said Axel hangs around with Memphis and I was to steer clear. Why?

He flashes me a toothy grin. "Now you came here for a reason. Want to train?"

My eyes flicker up to Gold, who's watching me right back. I need to get his attention. I need to prove to him I'm not just some prisoner, and the best way would be to put on a show.

"Yeah, give me someone I can fight. No offence but I'm pretty sure you'll crush me."

"Trouble, trouble, trouble, kid," Memphis almost sing-songs with a laugh, walking away.

I follow him over to the other side of the room and the row of mats littered on the floor.

"Dale, come and fight the new girl," he orders. "Don't piss your pants if she wins like you do with me."

"Seriously?" I mutter, eyeing the huge arms of the dude as he stalks over to the mat. He smacks his fists together, leering at me. Other than tight blue trousers, the guy doesn't have a shirt on, and usually, I would like the sight of a decent six-pack but his face ruins it. He's handsome, don't get me wrong, but I know a douche-canoe when I see one. It's all in his smug green eyes. Oh, this is going to be fun.

As predicted, Dale uses all his strength to tackle me head-on. I stay still, watching his foot movements and propel myself to the left, noticing that he prefers the right. Sure enough, he tumbles right past me and before he can pivot, I'm hot on his ass. I slam my fist into the centre of his neck, and he gasps as he reaches behind me, trying to grab my hair and ass, digging his nails in hard enough to break my skin.

Shit, that hurts.

I knee his back to stop him, and he falls like a plank under the pressure, not even able to stop his head smacking the mat. Unfortunately for him, his legs are open and when I knee him as hard as I can right between his thighs, a high-pitched screech leaves his lips. The poor guy doesn't even get up as Memphis claps and cheers, and so do a lot of the other prisoners who stopped to watch.

Breathless and panting, I look up to search the face of the only man that little fight was for.

Gold.

And he's smirking at me as he claps just once and inclines his head.

I've got his attention.

Step one complete for now.

Fuck, that felt so good!

Memphis wraps his arm around my shoulder. "Trouble, trouble, trouble, kid. You're playing with fire."

I laugh, keeping my voice low when I speak. "No, I'm playing with Gold."

CHAPTER SEVEN

Izora

"DINNER STARTED AN HOUR AGO, IZORA," Luke comments as his shadow fills the door of my cage and he slowly comes into focus. I ignore him, staring up at the ceiling, counting the dots of damp leaking through. How long before the water trickles its way onto my poor excuse of a bed? My back aches from sleeping on the paper-thin mattress. I've tried the padded floor, but it's just as poor.

Luke leans over me, his hands fisted at his side. "Move."

"I'm not hungry."

The sentence drifts between us and I can tell he isn't happy about the answer. To my surprise, he pushes my legs back and sits on the edge of my bed, looking at the cage wall.

"Not eating will make you sick," he warns me, his

attention still fixed on the wall. "And being sick doesn't get you out of here. They just let you die."

"I'm not starving myself, I just…" I pause, having no clue how to explain to Luke that I feel like giving up. I thought I could keep fighting and never surrender, but the more I think about it, there's no hope in this place. There's just death and cruelty. I'm not even sure what I'm going back to when I leave here in the end. The human world isn't bad exactly, but with no family, no work experience and no money, it's not going to be easy to get by.

"I know someone who might cheer you up. I'm not good at givin' anyone reasons to hope."

Turning my eyes to his for the first time since he sat down, I find a lot of sympathy and pity there. I almost hate this newfound pity of his. I hate that he doesn't see me as anything more than another prisoner.

"Then why keep trying?"

A frown flits over his face. "Would you rather I gave up on you, Izora?" He closes his eyes briefly. "I wish I saw you like a simple prisoner instead of the wild, silver-haired girl from the academy that I had a crush on once."

I blink at him, a little surprised by his comment.

"You had a crush on me?" I chuckle, not believing a word he says, though it's tempting. "I thought no one saw me next to Willow. She's the beautiful one."

He laughs, standing up and crossing his arms. "I never saw Willow because of you. I never saw anyone else."

I slide myself off the bed, feeling my cheeks burning a little as he nods to the door. He might actually be telling the truth. Well, shit. This changes things a little. It'll make Operation Unicorn easier, that's for sure.

"The new teacher is here," Luke says, standing off my bed, "and he personally requested to see you first."

"Why me?" Luke just shrugs at my question. "Fine, let's go then."

"Only if you promise to go to dinner afterward," he demands with an arched eyebrow.

"You drive a hard bargain," I mutter and he grins, nodding to the door.

I shake my head at him as we go out of my cage and down the steps to the main part of the prison. Luke leads the way to the other side, where there are rooms labelled 'education' and 'therapist'. It doesn't surprise me to know they have a therapist here. They even had one back at Shadowborn Academy. Turns out dying as a kid in dark magical water and becoming a shadowborn is a little bit haunting for anyone.

I'm glad I can't remember much. Or at least that was the excuse I gave for avoiding the academy's therapist, Gage, who's now my friend Sage's secret boyfriend. I wish I knew how my friends were doing. Luke knocks a few times on the education door and a deep, familiar voice states to come shortly after.

Luke holds the door open for me but doesn't come in once I step into the small classroom. My heart is in my throat when I see Professor Mune, a teacher from the academy who I was mildly obsessed with.

Okay, so mildly is putting it, well, mildly.

I had the biggest crush on this sexy beast of a man, but he never once noticed me. It feels like years ago when it's only been months.

Nothing has changed about Professor Mune since I last saw him. He's still a hot, rugged, silver fox even though his silver-dotted blue eyes don't seem at all that old. Just before I was kidnapped, he trimmed his beard down to a stubble, showing off more of his chiseled jaw and the handsome face that hid beneath. Now dressed in a tight black shirt with his sleeves rolled up his tattooed arms, black trousers that leave little to the imagination—thank the goddesses—he's as gorgeous as always.

A tear falls down my cheek, and I harshly wipe it away, breaking whatever moment there was here for a second. I'm just happy to see him. He's a light in an otherwise dark world.

"Are you okay?" His dark tone and pinched eyes make me shiver.

I cross my arms, taking two more steps closer to him. "Could be better, Professor Mune, not gonna lie."

"Call me Scott here." He also takes a step but then he pauses, and his expression darkens just like his tone. He leans against the desk and grips the sides with his large hands, his knuckles turning white. "I know you didn't do what they said you did. It's all bullshit, Izora, and I'm going to find a way to get you out."

My heart skips a beat at the words.

Fuck, if hearing my sexy *History of Magics* teacher talk like this isn't hot.

From the moment I entered his classroom at the academy and saw him, all rugged and bearded with his tattoos and silver hair, I wanted him. I planned to seduce him. Never in a million years did I expect him to come to my rescue.

"Why do you care about me so much?" I ask, furrowing my eyebrows in confusion.

"Let's just say my brother is here and he didn't do what he was accused of. He was the same age as you when he was falsely convicted." He grunts, running a hand through his slicked-back hair. "When I found out what happened here, I applied for a new part-time job. It was easy with Gage already working here once a week as the therapist."

"Gage as in Mr Michaels?" I ask incredulously, and Scott nods. "Is your brother still in here?"

He nods again, but his eyes make it clear I won't get a name.

"Once a week," he says in a dangerously low voice, "you will spend a day here with me. I plan to keep you safe at least for one day. Now, tell me what it's like in here. I'm not allowed to leave this room."

"Other than the Blood Trials, it's pretty normal."

"The Blood *what*?!" he all but roars. "You mean the ancient tradition the first Dark Fae King created? They are still doing that in *here*?"

Shivering, I think back to the line of bodies I saw. "Yep. They just treat the inmates like cuts of meat. It's brutal."

"It should have been stopped years ago, but I guess

Queen Narah doesn't want to end them or she would have."

I shrug at him, muttering. "Who knows what goes on in the minds of the fae?"

"Nothing good, that's for sure," he answers, his eyes intent on me.

"Wait. Do you know how Corvina Charles and Sage Millhouse are doing?" I question. "It must be year two for them now."

Something dark crosses his features. "Corvina Charles has made a name for herself. Did you know she was fae?"

"Corvina is *fae?*" I repeat, my eyes bulging in disbelief.

"Not just any fae. Why don't you sit down and I will tell you everything I know?"

I nod and drop into the seat by his desk, ready to hear what my friends have been up to.

By the end of the day, I know it's not just my life that's getting complicated.

It's my friends, too.

CHAPTER EIGHT

Izora

"**D**O YOU REALLY NEED TO FOLLOW ME everywhere all of the time?"

Luke flashes a wolfish grin as he holds my cage door open. "Not everywhere and not all the time."

I grumble at his retort. "It's not that I don't enjoy your company, but…" I slide by him, his scent invading my senses. "You constantly draw attention my way. Like, all the time. Also is that cologne I smell?"

"Au naturel," he says, closing the gate. "And good. Then they'll know not to come near you."

Au naturel, my ass. For some reason, he's put on some fancy spiced cologne today, and I can't help but wonder if it's for me. It'd mean my charm is beginning to rub off on him. His words from the other day play through my head, and I smile down at the floor as I follow him to the mess hall.

'I wish I saw you like a simple prisoner instead of the wild, silver-haired girl from Shadowborn Academy that I had a crush on once.'

I should really only feel relieved to know that a) he remembers me and b) sees me more than a prisoner. But I feel more than I should—excited, flattered, and giddy, to name a few. He also caught my attention at the parties. I just never expected him to notice me. I need to be careful with this Shadow Warden. He's still keeping me trapped here at the end of the day. Dammit. Why does my captor and, hell, even the governor, need to be sexy?

When we reach the hall, the two wardens who usually guard the doors are noticeably absent. Instead, there's a whole swarm of them hovering by the entrance. Not until I slide past a few of them do I realise what's going on.

They're preparing for the *Night of the Moon.*

"The festival is tonight?"

"Tomorrow," Luke corrects me, herding the way through the other wardens. "There will be a party here after sunset. The Gov's big on celebrating our holidays. This one is his favourite."

That certainly explains all the moon and star decorations hanging in the hall. The entire ceiling is being covered in them, and they're each moving and shimmering like the real night sky. I bet it'll look wonderful at night time. I wonder if we'll be allowed outside to bask in the moonlight? That's what the tradition calls for. It's the one day a year when there's a Blood Moon, and the whole forest celebrates it in honor of Selena, our Goddess of the Moon. Helios has a similar tradition, *Day of the Sun*, for their goddess Danica. They're both spectacular events, and for the first time since I arrived here, I'm a little excited.

I head over to the servery and grab some food. Much to my relief, Luke doesn't hang around like I was complaining about earlier. He actually gives me some space and talks to a colleague while I sit down to eat. I'm blissfully enjoying this moment alone when a looming shadow eclipses the corner of my eye.

I put my carton of juice down and look up at six beefy dudes towering over me. The guy I punched the other day is wearing a neck brace. Poor little baby. I almost laugh at how pathetic he looks. There's no way he really needs that. Even his suppressant collar is squeezing the foam which I bet isn't at all that comfortable.

What a fucking idiot.

But that's what he gets for touching my body without consent.

I look him up and down slowly. "What's wrong, handsome? Come back for round two?"

He steps forward, but the biggest of the group puts an arm out to stop him. This guy is at least a foot taller than the rest and his face is covered in scars, some of them superficial, but others, like the vertical one denting his cheek, are deep. His almond-shaped eyes flash towards me, one black and one blue.

"You think you're funny, don't you, fresh meat?"

I shrug casually, though inside my heart rate picks up. "I don't know about funny. I do have a good aim, though."

The guy's face contorts into an ugly smile. "Well isn't that something." His gaze flickers up to Luke and back again. "You won't always have your precious Shadow Warden around to protect you."

"That might be true," Axel growls, dropping into the stool on my left, "but she's got me. Go take your little mutts for a walk, Coen, and piss off. This one is ours."

Memphis steps around me and flaps a big hand dismissively. "Shoo the fuck away."

A strained silence stretches between the men. I half expect Coen to attack, but I remember what Luke said about Axel and Memphis ruling the roost, and right enough, Coen backs down. Casting me a generous glare, Coen and his cronies return to their chairs a few tables down.

Shuddering, I turn to the guys. "When you said 'this one is ours'—"

"We're claiming your sexy ass," Axel explains with not a flicker of hesitation.

My stupid heart skips a beat. "Why?"

"So none of those fuckwads will give you any hassle," he explains, throwing a sharp glare Coen's way. "They won't be bothering you no more."

I follow Axel's gaze. Coen is still staring at me. Honestly, I don't think he's stopped since he sat down. What a creepy guy.

"What does that make me to the two of you?" I ask, looking between them.

A wicked smile pulls at Axel's lips—one that makes my legs clench. "To me? Nothing you don't wanna be, cutie."

I grin at him, turning to Memphis. "What about you?"

He hesitates for a moment, then drags a hand through his hair. "I'm just looking out for you, kid. You're a good egg. I don't bat for that team, though, if you get my drift."

Dang it.

Figures he'd be off the table.

But Axel... now that's someone I'm definitely happy to hear about.

"Let's go, jaybird," Luke interrupts, just as the conversation is getting interesting. "Time to get you a job."

I push back from the table, nodding. "See you guys later."

Axel turns in his seat. "Hold up now. We're lookin' for a trainer," he says to me, causing the warden to stop in his tracks. "Just someone to help around and give those unlucky bastards a fighting chance in the arena. Think you're cut out for the job, kid?"

"I don't see why not," I say, glancing at Luke, who doesn't seem eager to agree.

"There are plenty of other jobs," he argues, clenching his jaw. "Safer ones."

The edge of Axel's lips twitch. "But they ain't got us. Why don't you let your *prisoner* decide, warden? After all, we get to pick our jobs, not you. Or are you taking that away from us now, too?"

Luke's hand quickly falls to his taser. Before things get ugly, I put myself between them.

"Come on, fellas. There's plenty of me to go around," I joke, but only Memphis acknowledges it with a grunt. "Maybe we can check the job out? If it's too dangerous, fine, I won't do it."

Luke finally peels his eyes off Axel and looks at me. After a strained pause, he nods. "All right. But you're not going alone."

The three of them walk me to the training room. It's already full of men and women fighting dummies and slamming each other onto the mats. Axel places his palm to the small of my back and a spark ripples through me.

"There are two arenas at this prison. One is where you go to train." He motions around the room, then points to where I know the auditorium is on the other side of the wall. "The other is where you go to die."

Memphis nods. "And while we can't save everyone who steps into the Blood Trials, we can at least give their sorry asses a chance by training them."

"Have you ever fought in the Trials yourself?" I ask curiously.

The muscles in Memphis' face harden. "The Fae Tryouts were enough for me."

I gape at him. "You competed in the tryouts? What happened? Did you win? My friends are competing this year. Guess I'll have to support them from here. What was it like? Give me all the deets."

"Later, kid. We've got jobs to do. Are you ready to help?"

I nod, a rush of excitement filling me. "Sign me up!"

Axel laughs. "At least she's enthusiastic."

"Go on." Memphis motions for me to join the others with a flick of his chin. "Let's see what you've got."

I look around the room, wondering where I should start. Most of the people here are working in pairs if not teams of three. Luke points me in the direction of the back of the room. There's a young girl trying her damnedest to fight one of the dummies. Even though it's only a hologram, it repeatedly outmaneuvers her, much to the surrounding wardens' amusement. I toss my braid over my shoulder and walk over, watching as she falls clumsily onto the floor.

"If this dummy was a dog, it'd be taking you for a walk."

She looks up at me, her brown eyes wide. "So? I still can't give up."

"And I admire that. Here…" I offer her my hand. She takes it and I pull her on her to her feet. Wow, she weighs practically nothing. How old is she? Fifteen at a push? That's way too young to be in here. "What's your name?"

"It's Abigail," she answers meekly. "Or Abbie. Whatever floats your boat."

"Nice to meet you. I'm Izora."

"I know who you are. You're the girl who knocked that guy out at the induction ceremony."

I can't help but laugh. "Yeah. You wouldn't think I'd be able to do that, just by looking at me, would you?" She shakes her head. "Looks can be deceiving. Many use it to their advantage. What are you good at?"

Her long, awkward pause doesn't fill me with much hope.

"Right. Umm. What's your weapon of choice?"

Abigail turns her back on me and watches the others kicking ass. "I'm not really a fighter."

No shit.

"Then why are you entering into the Trials?" I probe subtly, hoping there's still a way for her to back out. I can certainly give her some tips but I can't train her in a day.

At this rate, she won't last a second.

"Because my brother…" She hesitates, turning back to face me with tears in her eyes. "My brother died in the arena last week. He enlisted so he could get me out of here. I told him not to, but Kenneth, he…he was always so stubborn. I want to win so I can use my reward to get him a headstone."

"A headstone?" I repeat in a quiet voice.

"Life means nothing here and neither does death. They just burn the bodies once they pull them out of the arena. I *really* want to get him a headstone. He deserves that at least."

"Well…" I trail off, taking stock of how little chance this girl stands, and yet admiring her bravery at the same time. "I'll try my best to help. Let's get started…"

There's something harrowing about training people that may not live to see the next sunset. I spend most of the evening preparing inmates for the Blood Trials, and with every person I help, I wonder if I'll ever see them again. It's a little stupid, really. For all I know, they're locked up in here for the most vicious of crimes. And yet I wish them luck all the same before calling it a night.

My body aches from all the workouts. Luke lets me take a quick shower in the girl's communal bathroom before dinner. I hope the warm water helps to soothe my muscles, but when I step out and get dressed again, I'm still a bit tender. I think I overworked myself in the hopes to impress the guys, especially Luke and Axel. Axel spent quite a few sessions helping me train, and the way he watched me sent shivers down my spine. I so badly wanted to prove I'm cut out for the job. I just might have overexerted a little on the first day.

Back inside my cage, Luke hands me a tray of food for dinner, sparing me from the mess hall, much to my relief. I'm surprised to find two painkillers next to my glass of water. I slip the pills into my mouth and take a swig of water, grateful once again for Luke's kindness.

"What's on the agenda for tomorrow?" I ask him, digging into my bowl of food. Mmm, watery casserole. Just the way I like it. *Not.* I guess beggars can't be choosers, though.

"It's the festival. The party will start at dusk," Luke states, returning to his usual spot by the gate.

"When you say party…" I trail off, arching an eyebrow expectantly.

"No booze. He's not that generous."

"Damn."

Luke screws up his face, somehow making himself even sexier. "You really think it'd be a good idea to get all the inmates drunk? There would be a riot."

"Good point," I grumble. "Guess I was just wishful thinking."

"You're not at the Devil's Drop anymore, jaybird."

I finish off the last of my dinner, saying after a drink, "The best parties were always held there, weren't they? I miss them. Just being able to dance and forget everything."

The side of his eyes crinkle into a nostalgic smile. "Yeah. I miss them, too."

He takes my tray away and I watch him leave the room, wondering if I'll ever get to see that carefree side of Luke again.

CHAPTER NINE

Izora

I T'S TIME TO CELEBRATE THE LIFE AND DEATH OF our almighty goddess, Selena. Since it's a special occasion, I try to pick out the best outfit I possibly can. I pull on my tight grey jeans, a plain white blouse with a sweetheart neckline, and my tattered leather boots. I don't have anything silver to wear, which is usually customary during this festival. Oh well. I've done what I can. I finish the look off by unbraiding my damp hair and I let the soft curls drape down my back. A loose strand gets caught in my collar and I pull it out, looking over at the door as Luke enters again.

His gaze strays up and down my body, lust glittering within his cobalt eyes. "Are you ready?"

I give his own outfit a slow once over. He's wearing casual clothes this time, with his weapons still attached to the belt around his waist. His crisp white shirt is rolled up at the sleeves and held in place with a blood-red tie and matching braces. His dress trousers are dark like his shiny leather shoes, and I can smell his fancy cologne again. The bar holding his tie and shirt in place is silver, just like Selena's stars.

"Yeah," I reply, swallowing down my desire. "I'm good."

He opens the gate and motions me to come out. As I slip past him, I meet his gaze only to find that his eyes are rooted on my lips. An intense desire percolates between us, so powerful I can almost hear it cackling like magic. My stomach flips under his gaze. Falling for my prison warden? Not a good idea, Izora. Yet I can't seem to help myself.

I shake my head and follow him outside. The distant music carries to my ears. The corridor is filled with inmates making their way to and from the hall, with guards standing by at all times, ever silent and watchful. When we enter the hall itself, I'm surprised by the transformation. The decorations I saw at breakfast now adorn the walls and barred windows. The ceiling really does look like a sea of stars gleaming in the night sky. It's far too beautiful a display for a prison. The *Night of the Moon* really is Gold's favourite holiday.

I wonder what the other ones will be like? *The Feast of Zorya* is my personal favourite. It runs from the last day of winter to the first day of spring. When Selena and Danica were alive, they had a great feast on these days and both kingdoms came together to celebrate what had died in winter to make way for spring. I always enjoy it because it meant that even our darkest moments plant the seeds to new beginnings. It gives us hope. Sometimes hope is all we have to hold on to.

On the middle of the floor, surrounded by all the tables, stands a gigantic ice sculpture of Selena. Usually, these types of constructions display her planting the Evening Star into the sky. But this one shows her gazing into the *Fountain of Mene*, a look of tranquillity on her beautiful face.

Aside from the decorations and music, there doesn't seem to be much change, because everyone is doing what they usually do—eating at tables, playing games, placing bets, and trying to be heard over each other.

I turn to Luke, a tinge of pink gathering into my cheeks. "What do I do now? I've never been to a party in prison before."

Luke huffs a laugh and drags a hand through his slicked hair. "How about I get you a drink? Of fruit punch," he adds firmly, crushing that little glimmer of hope I had left.

"That'd be nice," I say, winking at him. "Always looking out for me, eh?"

He nods and makes his way over to the servery. There's a girl serving food this time. I've seen her a few times whenever Axel isn't manning the station. Beside the servery, there's a large table holding a punch bowl and a pile of plastic cups. Luke grabs two drinks, and I take another look around the hall, looking for the only other friends I have here. Speaking of the devil. Axel pops up at my side, offering me one of the red cups.

"You look parched, cutie. Drink up."

I take the drink from him, smiling my thanks. "You look…" I look him up and down. My mouth turns dry at how prominently his muscles are flexing under his tight grey dress shirt. God dang, it's practically hugging him. His black jeans are ripped at the knee, and his light blue suede boots really bring out his eyes. "Hot."

Axel's pupils dilate, and he wags his eyebrows. "Not too shabby yourself, cutie. I wanted to wish a sexy girl like you a Blessed Night."

The warmth that had claimed my cheeks moments before returns with a vengeance. I can feel the heat rise up my throat and assault my entire face. A 'Blessed Night' on this occasion is what people usually wish their loved ones.

"And to you, too," I reply sheepishly, willing the redness in my face to go away. "So how do you think I did yesterday? Am I part of the team?"

A proud smile dances over his face. "Memphis nearly shit his pants at how well you did. Thought maybe you'd be gunning for his job next." I give him a horrified look and he chuckles. "I'm kidding. We both knew you'd be a good fit. Ain't half bad, is it, training them? It kinda takes your mind off things. Makes you feel like you're doing something good."

He's right. When I was sweating away in the training room, I completely forgot about why I was here. I forgot about the fact that I don't have a life outside of all that and that I'm only here because I was framed. Helping my fellow inmates helped me drown everything out for a while.

I take a sip of my drink. "Have you ever fought in the Trials?"

Axel nods. "A few times."

I struggle to swallow the liquid down. "Did you kill anybody?"

"Yeah."

"How did it... like, feel?"

He pauses for a moment, considering my question. "It felt like shit, but it was either me or them, cutie. My face is too handsome to be rotting in a grave."

His laugh lightens up the mood a little and I smile. Across the hall, Luke is making his way back over with a frown on his face. I know he doesn't like it when I hang around Axel. He's just trying to protect me. But I have always been a good judge of character. It's one of the things that have kept me alive so far.

"Can I ask you a question, Axel?"

"Anything, cutie. Shoot away."

"What got you put in prison?"

A short pause stretches between us. Axel scratches his clean-shaven cheeks, his eyes pinched like he's contemplating whether or not to answer honestly or avoid the subject.

He releases a quiet breath and lowers his voice. "Would you believe me if I told you I don't belong here?"

"Yes. I don't think either of us belongs here. And I also don't think this prison is what it's cracked up to be."

My reply takes him by surprise and he widens his eyes, then narrows them again to scrutinize me closely.

"Then just know that whatever they tell you I did," he says in a low, gruff voice, "it's all lies, Izora. I didn't do shit to be trapped in here for the rest of my life. But every inmate says that, right?"

Luke halts beside me, eyeing my drink with a dispassionate glare. "I see Axel beat me to the punch."

His joke almost makes me laugh, if not for his sour expression.

"You know me, warden, I never like to see a lady without a drink," Axel practically sing-songs, his tone brightening. "While I have you here, I have a favour to ask."

Luke hands me the other drink and reluctantly slides out of earshot with Axel. I stand awkwardly for a moment until I spot Abigail. She's also on her own, slouched over the corner of a table and stabbing her food with her fork. I walk over and sit across from her.

"Thought I'd come to wish you good luck," I tell her, passing her the drink Luke gave me. "I just know you'll kick ass."

She nods absently, ignoring the drink and continues stabbing her food. I place the cup beside her. I really can't blame her sullenness. She's literally about to fight for her life in less than twenty-four hours.

"Is there a spot you'd like to place your brother's headstone once you win?" I ask softly, making sure not to say *if* she wins. "I noticed there's a cemetery by the front gate."

"That's just for wardens." She ponders for a moment,

dragging her food about her plate. "Kenneth liked to sit by this tree outside. You can actually see it from the window by the servery. I think I'll place it there."

I know just the tree she's talking about and it's a beautiful one. "I bet it's going to look wonderful there. It'll catch the sun in the morning."

Another nod, this time with a solitary tear slipping down her cheek. "Yeah. I've just gotta make sure I… I do it."

"You will. Don't start doubting yourself, Abbie. That's what the enemy wants you to do. Have every bit of faith in yourself like the other participants will have in themselves."

For the first time since I sat down, she smiles. It's weak but it's something. Catching sight of Gold entering the hall fashionably late, I return the smile and push away from her table.

I walk over to where Memphis is standing by the door, but I keep my attention on Gold, watching how he shakes hands with his employees and inmates like he really gives a shit about them. Anyone who endorses the brutality of the Blood Trials doesn't give a flying fuck about people. They only care about themselves. There must be a way to stop them. Inmates like Abigail don't stand a chance.

"Remember what I said about gunning for trouble, kid?" Memphis warns, dragging me from my train of thoughts.

"I was just wondering if there's a way to end the Trials, is all."

He follows my gaze over to Abigail who's now dumping her untouched meal into the bin. A guilty knot coils in my stomach like a snake. I pretty much lied to her about winning. What was I supposed to say? *Yeah, you're gonna die, Abbie, but I'm praying to Selena it'll be swift.* Prayers won't do anything to save her or the others forced to play this barbaric game.

Memphis gently squeezes my shoulder. "She's not the first and she won't be the last. First rule of being a trainer, kid—don't get attached. It's not our job to worry about who'll make it out alive. We just gotta give them some pointers and hope they'll use them wisely to reach the other side. You get me?"

"I know, and I do, it's just so cruel." I sigh, frowning at Gold chatting away with a group of guards, a stupid big smile on his face. I hate how fucking sexy he looks in his navy suit. "There must be something I can do."

Memphis is quiet for a long moment, rubbing his chin in thought. "Unless you can get close to Gold and persuade him to stop them, there isn't nothing you can do."

Gold slides me a veiled glance, cold and calculating, but there's something sinister behind it...something dangerous. It's like he can hear our conversation from the other side of the hall. Goosebumps break out over my skin and a shudder racks through my body. Getting close to this man may be my only bet. I'm no stranger to playing dirty to get what I want, and I want freedom more than anything. I also want to put an end to the Blood Trials.

I turn back to face Memphis, and we talk about my

first day at work. It's a relief to hear I did a good job, and for once, didn't fuck up. Axel returns with fresh drinks and I take a sip of mine.

"Miss Dawn. I believe we have yet to meet in person," Gold says, his breath ghosting my ear ever so lightly.

I nearly spit my drink back out. He's standing right beside me. And this close up, his eyes are both terrifying and mesmerising. The vertical irises, bathed in a field of gold, are intent on my own. Not even Zander's eyes are quite this unnerving. I find it hard to look away. All I can do is listen and watch as he turns to my friends.

"Axel, Memphis. I'd like to discuss something with Izora in private."

The guys exchange a tense glance. It's Axel who makes the first move, followed by a sulking Memphis.

"Be careful," Memphis whispers in my ear, stepping around me.

"Gold's a *snake*," Axel adds without an ounce of subtly.

The insult only amuses the governor, who curves his lips into a derisive grin. He watches the guys move away and only when they're out of earshot does he turn to me.

"I'm really not as bad as they make out," he says.

Oh, I beg to differ, I want to spit back but I just manage to stifle the words. Is this handsome bastard deluded? He's a monster as far as I'm concerned.

"We're all misunderstood at times," I reply instead, inwardly cringing at how sincere I sound.

"As I believe Tyler found out on Tuesday when he broke one my rules," he remarks, his grin spreading into a smile. "You gave him quite the wake-up call. You are certainly not someone to be misunderstood, are you?"

"No... sir."

"Sir?" He chuckles dryly. "Look, Izora, I think we both know I'm not your sir yet. Governor or Gold will do."

I pick up on the word 'yet'. What's that supposed to mean? My eyes sweep over the tattoos on his face. I can't make any of the symbols out. They must be some ancient language of the forest. Maybe Draconian? I wouldn't be surprised. He has dragon eyes, after all.

Gold catches me staring and grins. "You know, I'm very intrigued to see how you would fare in the arena. The Blood Trials may be barbaric to some, but to others, it's the only way to survive this prison. I know that more than anyone."

Somehow, I doubt that. It's not like *he's* ever competed. He just likes to watch the blood paint the grounds of his arena like a canvas.

"The Trials is clearly something you take great pride in," I say, trying to come across genuinely interested in him and his sick hobby.

"It... is the way things have been since King Ares ascended the Throne of Luna." Gold's flicker of hesitation surprises me. "The Blood Trials was his way of claiming Zorya. He would select the victors as his warriors. It used to be a great honor."

"But what happens to the victors now?" I demand, just managing to hide the scorn in my voice. "Do they become warriors or do they just wait until the next bloodbath?"

A dark glint flashes in his eyes. He glances up at the ceiling and then back to me again, his eyebrows knitted together. "Many traditions start with blood. It's not only our world that has them but the human realm and those beyond."

That doesn't make it any better.

However, it seems the only way to impress Gold is to win the Blood Trials. That's all he clearly cares about. I don't think I'll be able to get close to him any other way. Plus, if I do make it out alive, there are some upsides. I'll not only hold Gold's attention, but I'll also gain rewards. Those rewards could be useful here for sure. All I need to do is stay alive. I'm fast and good at hiding. I'm also light on my feet and can knock a six-foot guy into the middle of next week. Surely I've got it in the bag?

Yes, the so-called tradition repulses me.

But competing might be the only way for my plan to work.

"Maybe I need to compete first before giving an opinion," I say, folding my arms across my chest. "You know, to get a better understanding of this… tradition."

Gold's face lights up with wicked intent. "Perhaps you should compete."

He says the words casually, but I can tell by his pupils that he's excited. This is exactly why he came over here. He wants me to play his game. But is he ready for me to win?

"Not only compete, sir. I'm going to win," I tell him. "Just you watch."

He gives a swift, abortive laugh. "Now *this* is what I'm looking for. Good luck, Izora. I look forward to watching you tomorrow in the arena. May Selena protect you."

I don't need Her protection. I've got revenge on my side and that's the only backup I need to make sure I beat Gold at his own game.

The governor inclines his head and returns to mingling with his prisoners. It's all a little sick, really, watching him chat with everyone like they're not being caged here by his command. I swallow the last of my drink, throw the cup into a bin, and head towards the exit at the other end of the hall. I pass Coen and his cronies along the way, who each give me a very generous glare. I'm not surprised to see the warden that brought me to this prison is sitting with them. I am surprised, however, to find Janis and Sharon Roth sharing the same table. The two of them fawning over Coen, who couldn't look more disinterested even if he tried. I knew there was a reason I didn't take to those girls immediately.

"Where do you think you're goin'?" Luke demands, his hand landing on my shoulder. He spins me around so that I'm forced to look up at him, and his cheeks are a little pink.

"I'm going to sign up for the Blood Trials."

My response doesn't go down well with him; I suspected as much. The blood drains from his face and he narrows his eyes into shards of ice.

"You're... *what?*"

I squirm a little in his grip, averting my gaze from his.

"You heard what I said. I get the same rights as everyone else here, right? I get to choose whether or not I want to participate in the Trials?"

Instead of answering, he digs his fingers into my arm and drags me from the hall. I expect him to stop in a quiet corner somewhere nearby, but he keeps on walking all the way up the stairs, through empty halls and towards the back right corner of the prison. I stumble in his wake, trying to keep up as he drags me through a cold, dark room. Another secured door later and we enter an even colder room. The air claws at my lungs like ice, and when Luke switches on the lights, my breath streams out before me. This room stinks of antiseptic. It's suffocating.

"Where are we?" I question, scanning the sterile-white room. When my gaze lands on the autopsy table and the body contained inside a transparent incubator, bile rises into my throat. That alone answers my question. But why did he bring me here?

"You wanted to sign up for the Blood Trials?" Luke sneers, walking over to the cabinets stacked against the wall. He swipes his pass down various keypads and reaches into each of the cabinets. "I thought I'd show you what happens to most of those that do. Look at them. *Look*!"

I unclench my eyes and gaze down at all the dead bodies. Some of them are stitched up and already decomposing, others are clearly not finished having their bodies assessed yet.

"They're only kept here until they're harvested. Once

their organs have been ripped out, they're thrown into a pit and burned with the others."

I flinch, my insides recoiling. I remember Abigail telling me the same thing. Tears sting my eyes just looking at the bodies. He's pulled out at least ten of them, but I bet every one of those huge cabinets is filled with corpses. Filled with people who desperately wanted a better life in this prison.

"This doesn't change my mind," I say quietly, peeling my gaze off the bodies.

He gawks at me as if he thought I'd be so utterly repulsed by the bodies that I'd change my mind.

"Why? Why would you wanna go in there? It's suicide."

"It's a chance," I counter quickly, looking right at him. "I know what I'm doing, Luke. If you're so against the Blood Trials like I am… trust me on this."

"Trust you?" he whispers, stepping back. "You can't stop the Trials. Nobody can."

That's not quite right—Gold can stop them. Working my way through him is part of my plan.

Luke waves his hand and the bodies roll back into their cabinets, the sound echoing loudly around the room. I close the space between us.

"Just trust me, Luke? Please?"

After a long, strained moment, Luke sighs in resignation and reaches out to me. My breath hitches as I think he's about to caress my face, but his hand lowers onto my shoulder, and the air is sucked from my lungs.

Darkness envelops us. The shadows wrap around our bodies, and then we're standing outside a room called 'PROCESSING ROOM'.

"If I can't stop you… This is where you sign up."

I smile at him, strangely relieved by his acceptance. I shouldn't care about my warden's acceptance or not. I shouldn't care about a lot of things. But I do feel more at ease knowing he's not going to hate me once I get out alive.

Wrapping my hand around the door handle, I take a deep breath, then pause to look back at Luke.

"Thank you," I say, "for trusting me."

And with that, I step into the room to sign my life away again. I have no intention of dying in the arena tomorrow—only winning.

CHAPTER TEN

Izora

MY HEART FEELS LIKE IT'S GOING TO BEAT OUT of my chest in the small walk from my cage to the door that leads to the Blood Trials and beyond. Thankfully, there is a group of about twenty around the doors, all of them staring ahead with their heads held high, not an ounce of fear displayed on their faces. I spot Abigail at the front, and she's as white as a ghost. I can only pray that Selena will be with her. I stop not far from the group and glance back to see Luke has stopped in the middle of the room. His eyes are cold and haunted with indecision on how he can stop me from doing this.

I want to tell him it's all going to be okay, but lying isn't worth it and he's too smart to believe me anyway. Luke can't protect me when I step through these doors. In fact, no one but myself can do that. And protecting myself is exactly what I intend to do. Surviving this round is my target. Impressing the governor my mission.

I steel my back and turn around, crossing my arms as I wait for the doors to open. It almost feels like I'm a gladiator, waiting for the moment I step out into the arena to fight for my life. I guess it's a little true. A mechanical buzz sounds overheard as the doors swing apart and the group heads inside. I follow last, stepping into the cold room, and the doors snap shut behind me like the lid on a coffin.

The Shadow Warden who brought me to this prison is standing waiting for us. He looks every bit the stern military man in his ebony uniform with his taser held at his side like a cane. A new gold badge on his collar has his name inscribed: Warden Kyle. That's a name I'll surely never forget.

"Welcome to the Blood Trials." He gestures around the hall but doesn't bother pointing to the arena. I suppose he doesn't have to since most of us have already seen what happens down there. "This is a tradition created by the fae kings and queens of old. It is meant to test the strength of those who are imprisoned for their crimes. If you win the first round, you will pass into the second and final one that will decide your fate. This round, however, will test your endurance and innovation skills. A pack of fellow inmates will be joining you inside, but be warned. Their goal is to obtain this and the only way to do so is by killing you."

He flicks his hand in a circular motion, and a glowing red orb swings around his finger.

"You will each have an orb like this that will be magically bound to you and your power. The object of the game is easy: obtain as many orbs as you can and the three survivors at the end will win. It's blood for blood here in this arena, so don't give any mercy when none shall be shown to you. There are no rules. No repercussions. You can do anything to win. Play dirty for all we care, yet keep it entertaining. We have fae watching."

I follow his gaze to the top corner of the arena, where Gold and a flock of aristocrats are watching through a magical shield. I'm not surprised to find out Gold is fae. His incinerating eyes search the faces of the group, and when they land on me and the corner of his lips turn into a smile, my stomach clenches.

"Why do the fae want to watch us?" I mutter quietly, but Warden Kyle catches my words.

"Figure it out yourself," he snaps.

I get the feeling he will never tell me the answer and anything as simple as they like to watch death doesn't make sense. I've heard the courts of the fae have enough death, pain and pleasure to put the mortal world to shame. Maybe this is just another perverse game of theirs?

Warden Kyle waves his hand and the orb disappears into thin air. "As for rewards… Well, if you put on a good enough show, you might get everything you'll ever need in Shadowborn Prison. You may even get to join the governor's pack."

I grin. That is exactly what I want.

"So there's your incentive. Now, turn around and get ready. You have five minutes."

I turn around to see various walk-in lockers with our names on them. I open the door to my own one and step into a freezing cold room. On the wall is a white catsuit and matching trainers on the floor. I quickly strip off and pull the catsuit on. The material is super tight yet flexible, but it's not going to leave much to the imagination, especially not with my black sports bra and panties. Once I pull the shoes on, the door on the other side slams open and I walk through it.

I enter a room with stacks of weapons piled high on the tiled floor. The other inmates are scrambling to get the best ones. I rush over, finding a belt full of knives, and I clip it around my waist. I sift through the pile and grab two magical guns which I've only ever seen on the hips of the prison wardens. I know one shot from these will instantly kill you. I clip them onto my belt and by the time I look back, the only thing on the ground is an old-looking machete, but it will do. Lastly, I find a chest sword holder near the back of the room and wrap it around my chest before sliding the sword into it on my back.

Once everyone has geared up and we wait for the next step, I eye the room we are in and the inmates I'm going to have to beat for this to work. The room is circular on one side and the other has a row of twenty lockers. The spherical part of the room has at least thirty holes with steel doors shut against them, making me wonder what the hell they are for. I instantly spot a problem when four of the biggest guys huddle together and start talking. They weren't gathered outside so I can only assume they are the inmates the warden warned us about. Fuck. And they also happen to be the ones who challenged me at breakfast—minus the guy I punched in the throat. Coen's gaze lands on me and I look away, contemplating my nails as if his existence means nothing to me. I hear him chuckling, and I know for sure he'll be gunning for me the moment the game begins. Either I take him out first, or I run as fast as I can. I guess I'll make my decision once we enter the arena.

As for the rest of the inmates, they're a complete mixture. Some of them I wonder why they would enter this thing in the first place, especially the one boy with curly red hair that looks no older than sixteen. And then there's Abigail. Sweet little Abigail. She's managed to wield a sword rather impressively, but the tiny gun attached to the holster on her hip won't hold many rounds. I hope she thinks on her feet and runs the second this all kicks off.

From a speaker somewhere in the room, a loud countdown begins. It counts from fifty down to zero, and then the steel doors of the holes pull open. Hovering within each of them is a red orb made of glass that shimmers with dark magic.

A mechanical female voice fills the room. "Welcome to the first round of the Blood Trials. Take an orb and slide down the hole once the countdown stops. May the goddess Selena be with you."

I don't need telling twice.

I rush to the hole in front of me, wrapping my hands around the orb. It immediately zooms to my leg, attaching itself to my thigh and shrinking in size. I turn my leg to the side to see tiny holes in a line going down and I'm guessing that's how I hold the orbs. The countdown continues until we get to the final part.

Three.

Two.

One.

I hold back a scream as air sucks me into the hole before I can let go, and I fly straight down, falling straight out into the open air. A pained gasp gets stuck in my throat as I bounce into what feels like a net and my body rolls into a stop. Eventually, I tip off the side of the net and smack onto a pile of thick wet leaves. Well aware that the others are aiming to kill me, I jump up and look around just as a guy rolls off the net and lunges for me. He falls on top of me, and I scream, more out of shock than anything, and wrestle him to the ground. His hand wraps around my throat as his other one reaches for the sword on his back. I slide a knife out of my belt, my lungs begging for air, and all I can do is slam my dagger into his throat. His blood gushes out onto my face and his eyes widen into lifeless plates as he falls off me, coughing blood everywhere.

My entire body is shaking. I'm all adrenaline right now, and that's all I really need. I quickly assess the air and I'm relieved to see that I'm alone as far as I'm aware. The landscape looks like a rainforest and everything feels so real, from the exotic bird calls cloying the dense air, to the droplets of water raining down from the canopies. I look back to the listless body splayed at my feet. He isn't the first guy I've killed, and should I need to defend myself here, he won't be my last.

A sliver of guilt lodges in my throat as I tear his orb from him and stick it to my thigh. I also take his sword since he won't be using it and clip it to my back, then I stand and take a deep inhale of the air. The intense warmth of the rainforest is stifling. It's insane how realistic this place is despite only being a simulation. It's just magic twisted into a game I intend on winning. I glance down at my now blood-covered suit and shake my head. No matter how flexible and waterproof the material is, this is the worst thing to wear in a place where I'm being hunted. There's nothing discreet about it.

I dart into the trees. My shoes sink into the soft earth as I look around for a tree big enough to temporarily hide me. I find one and quickly sink down into its damp leaves. I dig through them to the wetter mud below and grab a handful. I rub it all over my catsuit, hoping to provide a bit of much-needed camouflage. Once I run the mud through my silver hair, I draw three lines on my cheeks for luck and stand up.

Time to go hunting.

Digging out two daggers, I trek through the forest, staying close to the trees. I wonder if I should climb them to get a better angle, but then I hear a long, echoing growl that is way too loud for my liking. By the time I turn around, a monstrous tiger pounces off the tree, its claws going straight for my throat. I don't have time to be scared or think about my decision. I let instincts take over and shift into my snow-white wolf, knowing this is a fight for her. She bursts out of me in pure, undulating fury and pounces up to meet the tiger in midair.

They clash like a storm.

The tiger's claws dig into her hide as she takes a chunk of flesh between her fangs, tasting blood in her mouth. This creature might be huge, but my wolf is bigger, and she uses every ounce of weight and strength to overpower it onto the ground. Clawing and gnawing her way to victory, she lands on top of the beast and tears out its throat in one bite, her huge paws bathed in its blood. With a long howl, she shifts back, and I nearly fall to my knees from all the cuts covering my body. Fortunately, I'm not deeply wounded and adrenaline is helping to stifle the pain right now. I look over at the dead tiger just as it slowly bursts into a cloud of dust. It was clearly only part of the simulation and not real, which meant its efforts weren't a match for my wolf. I have a feeling she'll be helping me out a lot during this fight. I straighten off the ground after a long, deep exhale, and smudge more mud over my clothes.

"Did you hear that? It was this way!"

Shit. Those voices are close.

I grab the daggers I dropped during my shift before running in the opposite direction of the voices. The good thing about being small and petite is my footsteps are light and I'm mindful of my breathing and every noise that I make. I listen for any sounds that don't seem quite right. The sound of water rushing over rocks sticks out the most, and I come to a halt. Water is usually the best place to start in a situation like this, right? I follow the sound and step out of the trees toward a truly breathtaking waterfall.

Unfortunately, I'm not alone as a trio of boys emerges from the other side. They must be working together to steal as many orbs as they can. One of them already has five attached to his leg. They smile when they see me and run into the water, wading their way through. I search around for an escape just before I hear their screams. I look back to see them all frozen, screaming in agony as gigantic eels wrap around their legs. The boys scream and beg for my help while the eels slither up their bodies, eventually wrapping around their necks and popping their heads like crushes melons.

Okay. The water is deadly.

Got it.

All of them are suddenly pulled under the water and then five orbs float out a second later. They hover for a moment before shooting towards me and attaching themselves to my legs. That's seven orbs now, including my own. Surely that would put me in the top three of the winners?

"Right. I need to hide until the end," I whisper to myself, looking around for a tree to hide in.

I spot a big enough one not far from here and I run over to it, using one of my knives to help me climb. But the bark is actually quite thick and uneven, which makes it easier than I thought it would be to climb. I pass four branches before I find a heavy one that has a good vantage point over the rainforest below. Even though this is all fake, my heart still hurts for those three dead guys and the tiger. I know the tiger wasn't real but those guys definitely were. I remember seeing them in the armory.

Please, Selena, say none of this is real.

I spend time checking out my cuts, noticing that other than three lines on my ribs, the rest have stopped bleeding and will heal quickly. The one on my ribs might need something. I rip my sleeve with my knife and cut it so it makes a long bandage before wrapping it around my ribs, stopping the bleeding for now.

A far-off cry in the distance is swiftly silenced, the sound chilling me to my core.

"Please leave me alone! Yo-you can have it!"

The girl's pleading is filled with desperation, and a feeling of dead twists my stomach as I register who the voice belongs to.

Abigail.

I look down to see the girl I was training just a few days ago. She's standing in the bushes, holding her orb up to a pack of wolves in surrender. The four of them stand in a line, their black fur bristling from the shadow magic that shimmers around them. Where's the alpha? I know there's supposed to be five of them, including Coen. The wolves growl and snap at Abigail as she throws the orb at them and turns to run. Just as I go to jump down and help her, I'm already too late. An enormous brown wolf, littered in scars and blood that oozes down its throat, emerges from the shadows. It must be Coen judging by his mismatched eyes. He lands on top of Abigail and rips her to pieces before my eyes. Her screams fill the air as the other wolves join in and tear her limb from limb. I cover my mouth with my hand before my scream can escape and turn away, tears falling down my cheeks as I silently scream into my palm.

Bright white light blasts against my eyes and a rush of cold air sweeps around me as I suddenly fall to the ground. The tree I was in is now gone. An empty black room surrounds me. My chest feels like it's going to explode as I try to catch my breath. I look around, and there, not ten feet away, stands Coen, decked out in orbs just like the rest of his pack. He's holding what remains of Abigail and he's smiling at me, his face covered in her blood. His tongue pokes out like a viper and licks the residue from his lips. I want to kill him. I want to slit his throat with my own blade and take down every member of his pack. But my adrenaline is beginning to wear off, and a woozy sensation takes hold of me.

I don't remember hearing the cheers of inmates or the governor clapping before heading back to my cage. I don't even notice that Luke isn't here. I just shut my cage door, peel off my bloodstained clothes, and crawl onto my bed. I've seen a lot of things in my eighteen years. Never have I seen so little regard for magic life. And for what? Sport? Entertainment? Abigail was right—life and death are truly meaningless in this world. We're just pawns of puppeteers. We mean nothing to the fae that cage us. At this rate, I'll never make it out of here alive. There's got to be a way to put an end to the Blood Trials…

A sharp pain stings me on my stomach and I snap awake. My eyes tumble into Luke's sitting on the edge of my bed, his cold fingers hard at work on my ribs, gently rubbing a thick oil into the cuts.

"They are infected, and shit, you don't deserve to die that way," he whispers softly, but then in the blink of an eye he stands and clears his throat.

I feel like he's always fighting with himself about whether he should like me or not.

I straighten up, grabbing my shirt off the floor and pulling it over me. "Thanks."

He nods once. "I also bought you dinner from the governor."

I follow his gaze to the box at the bottom of my bed. I did wonder what the nice smell was. I gently reach over and open the box, discovering a selection of cakes at the top. When I pull them out there is a roast dinner concealed in a plastic tray underneath. Actual food. I almost drop the box in shock. *This is from the governor?*

"Eat up. I have a surprise reward for you later," Luke instructs, pushing off the bed.

"Reward?" I echo, my stomach grumbling despite the atrocities of the arena still plaguing my mind.

He raises a brow. "Surprise reward."

I sit back on my bed and smile weakly at him, trying to push the bloody memories from my mind. He steps outside the cage, his back facing me, leaving me to eat my food. I'm surprised by how hungry I am and I practically wolf everything down. I do feel a little better after eating. Opting to leave the cakes for later, I stand up and walk over to Luke, who steps aside to let me out. He's silent most of the way down the corridor.

"Did you see the Blood Trials?" I ask as we head through the main part of the prison. He doesn't answer me but I come to a halt just as five familiar-looking men walk past with the piles of bodies from the arena. They've just dumped them into a bunch of wheelbarrows like they're nothing. I spot Abigail's blond hair poking out from the plastic sheet. Tyler, the guy I throat punched, sniggers as he wheels her past.

"I watched every second," Luke answers, pausing to glare at them, Coen in particular, who looks like he's just won the fucking lottery. "Some people are born evil, Izora."

He takes my arm, but before he drags me away, I tell him, "And some people have the gods behind them when they get revenge for the fallen."

I look intently at him, waiting for him to say something. He just takes me down a long, empty hallway, and towards a door that says 'WARDENS ONLY'.

"Revenge is a road you don't wanna go down," he warns, making sure to catch my gaze.

I frown right back at him. Revenge and wanting to

be free is all I have left now. "You might be my warden out here. But who says you can tell me what to do in the arena?"

"Stop talkin'," he snaps, and a flash of magic flickers in his eyes.

It makes me smile to know that I can get him close to losing his shit. He waves his hand over the lock and the door pops open. The cool evening air brushes against my skin, and I take a deep inhale, savouring the freshness. Two guards on the other side nod at Luke before they head back through the door. It closes behind them with a loud thud, and I look up at the high-gated field we are stood in.

"What we are doing out here?" I ask him softly.

Luke holds his pass to the front of my collar, and it beeps. "You have an hour to shift and run about. Don't bother shiftin' into a bird of any sorts, or tryna to escape, because they will shoot you out of the sky."

For a second, I'm in complete shock, touched by his kindness. The moment doesn't last long though before my wolf demands to be set free.

I so badly want to be free, too.

Allowing my wolf to take over, we shift effortlessly and she takes off across the field, running and frolicking in the wet grass. Even in a cage, there are moments of freedom it seems.

CHAPTER ELEVEN

Izora

"C AN I HAVE A MOMENT WITH HER?" I HEAR Axel ask my warden in an uncharacteristically nice voice.

That isn't normal for him.

I look up from where I'm sitting on my bed, and Axel is all up in Luke's space. Ah, nice voice, scary as shit face. Of course. Now that makes more sense.

"Luke…" I gently say, and my voice snaps them both out of it.

The warden moves aside and turns his back to the cage. Axel grins and jumps on the bed beside me, holding a plastic cup of fruit.

"Axel, did you come here to cause trouble?"

His naughty grin says it all, really.

"I wanted to wish you good luck and hope that I see you on the other side," he answers honestly.

"Have you won before?"

"Sure, but I'm special. I saved the Gov's life once and earnt a damn good room and protection."

Interesting. I wonder if Axel could be another way of getting close to Gold. I know I shouldn't use him like that, but I have to get myself out of here. I'm sure I could convince Gold to take Axel with us anyway.

Axel throws a blueberry into his mouth and chews. "And, little miss trouble, you best get any thoughts of using me to get Gold's attention out of your pretty little head."

Shit. Can he read my thoughts or something?

"You think I'm pretty?" I say around a grin. "How sweet."

"Don't fuck up today. I'm getting used to seeing your very pretty face around here," he whispers in a more serious tone, leaning closer to kiss my cheek.

Heat rises into my face, and my grin turns into a coy smile. It's wiped away when Luke smacks his baton on the cage door.

"No touchin' other inmates! You know the rules, Axel."

Axel winks at me as he stands up, taking his time to lazily stretch his arms. I fully appreciate the view for a moment before he walks past Luke, whispering something that I can't hear but it really, really pisses Luke off. I jump off my bed, rushing over and blocking his view of Axel walking away.

"Luke, aren't we meant to go to the Blood Trials for round two?"

"Yeah," he mutters, shaking his head and storming off without me.

Men.

This is a prime example of why I've only ever had one boyfriend, who took my virginity and two weeks later I found him in bed with my step-sister. After that experience, I decided guys my age weren't a good idea and then I moved to Shadowborn Academy where every guy only had eyes for my step-sister anyway. The fucking irony.

If Willow was here, I'm sure I'd be forgotten about as per usual. Then again, Luke's comment about never seeing Willow flickers into my mind and I almost pause mid-step. Maybe I was choosing to only see the bad in every guy I ever spoke to?

I certainly did with Luke, and now he's here protecting me when we both know he must have better things to do. He might be my warden but that doesn't make him my babysitter. He's always around me. He's always *worried* about me. I stay a few feet away from Luke all the way to the doors of the arena, which are strangely open even though we are early. Luke comes to a halt a few inches away from the door and I go to walk past him but his hand shoots out and grabs my wrist.

"You're too good to die in a place like this."

I step closer, well aware I shouldn't with all the cameras around. "That's the problem, Warden Luke. You think I'm good when I'm not. I've been bad since I was born and the world always knew it. In this prison, I'm figuring out that maybe I knew it all along, too. The only difference between good and bad is the person the title belongs to."

I tug his arm away, ignoring the shock in his eyes.

"You didn't kill those wardens, did you?"

His voice is like a whisper sinking its way into my ears even as I get to the door. I only look back once, knowing I'll see Luke's broken eyes.

I put on a brave face and smile at him. "Oh, Luke, you know the answer to that or you wouldn't be my friend!"

I don't get to hear his reply as the door slams shut behind me and the second round of the Blood Trials begins.

After being shoved into a locker, I find a bunch of clothes and weapons suitable for snow. The thick, fur-lined jacket, snow boots, and insulated trousers are a dead giveaway even if the pickaxe wasn't. Clipping on my belt of knives, I carry the pickaxe out into the room that had all the weapons last time. There aren't any other players this time. I guess they all died in the last round. That means my only opponents are Coen and his wolves.

A woman's voice, the same one from the last recording, starts to speak.

"Welcome to the second round of the Blood Trials. In this round, you will be tested on not only your survival skills but your luck. To win, you must find the ice that cannot be missed in the snow. If the gods favour you, you will survive and be blessed beyond your wildest dreams. May Selena herself watch over you."

The steel door of one of the holes snaps open, and there is a blue orb floating in the middle. As soon as I step closer, it flies to me, attaching itself to my leg and shrinking in size all over again. I sit on the edge of the hole before closing my eyes and pushing off, tumbling straight down until the freezing cold air assaults my lungs. I gasp from the shock as the hole spits me out at full speed and I drop into the snow face first.

Ouch.

The sound of someone laughing hurts a little more. Mysterious laughing is never a good sign. I sit up and blink through the thick snow, instinctively grabbing one of my knives.

"You dropped this."

A grimace up at the tall guy overshadowing me, dropping my pickaxe into the snow in front of me. He's cute, enough that most girls would drop their knickers in a moment's notice. I grab the pickaxe and quickly jump to my feet, pinning the sharp edge right under his neck. He doesn't move as I look into his piercing grey eyes. He looks somewhat familiar with his shaggy brown hair. My eyes fall onto the scar on his lip and stray down to his clothes. He has similar winter items to what I'm wearing, so I know he's another player in the Blood Trials. When I see the green orb on his leg, I know I should kill him. But I hesitate. *Why am I hesitating?*

"Kill me when we both get to the end," the boy says,

raising a machete in supplication. "What's the point of trying to kill me now and losing help?"

The statement makes me halt more than his commanding voice. He even sounds familiar, but I don't know where I've heard him before. Either way, I haven't seen this guy around the prison and he's hardly easy to miss.

"How can I trust you not to stab me in the back, pretty boy?" I growl, pushing the pickaxe just a tad harder. The vein in his throat pulses under it, threatening to release blood.

"Take my weapons," he suggests, his smooth tone without a scrap of fear.

"You could still strangle me," I resort. "Nah, I think I had the right idea the first time."

"Wait!" His command stops me for a moment. He reaches up, wrapping a hand around the end of the ax and pushing until thick drops of blood drop onto the snow. The wind picks up my hair, blowing it at my side as I watch him hold his hand in the air. "I swear on Selena to not harm you until we find the end of this trial."

The blood promise is binding, everyone knows that. The gods might not be around anymore, but their magic definitely is. Anyone that breaks a blood promise ends up going crazy or their magic eats them alive from the inside out.

One or the other, and neither of them are pretty.

With a deep sigh, I lower my weapon and tug my eyes away from him. It's clear we are on a mountain from a quick glance around. The pressured feeling in my chest says we're near the summit. I get a feeling we need to head down rather than up. Why else would they drop us off more than halfway up? If the end of the trial took place on the summit, it wouldn't provide much entertainment for the fae since it'd be over too soon. No, I think we're supposed to head south. The landscape is definitely the last I expected Gold to pick. At least the air is warm unlike the snow itself. Good thing, too, because my kit didn't have any gloves. It'd make wielding my weapons all the harder and so would frostbitten hands.

"What's your name?" I ask, spotting a line of trees not far away. Odd for this far up a mountain. We should stay in the tree line to avoid the other players the best we can.

"Alexander, or Alex. You?"

Nice name for a pretty boy. "Izora, but call me Iz."

I don't wait for him as I wade through the thick snow towards the trees, only slowing down when the trees cover us. I hold on to the trees for support to stop myself slipping down, and the rough bark scrapes against my palms.

"So why are you in the Blood Trials, Iz?"

I turn back, seeing that Alex is well and truly keeping up with me.

"I want a nicer room," I lie, and he chuckles.

"I'm going to ask you once not to lie to me," he warns and I stop, facing him. "The next time you lie, you will not like what I do next."

"Don't like lies?" I slide him a glance, not quite buying that. "Even sweet little white lies that do nothing but keep people happy?"

117

"I hate lies, period. That's my truth," he snaps, stepping past me. I follow behind him. "Tell me your truth. Something you don't tell anyone else."

"I was never loved by anyone," I answer, the words spilling out of my mouth. I try to catch them but I just… keep talking. I suppose if I'm going to open up to anyone, it'd be someone I need to kill later. "My mum put up with me but every time she looked at me, I never saw love. I saw obligation, possibly loyalty to her blood, but not love. My step-father, my step-sister and everyone in my life have always seen right past me like I'm not there. Some days, back home, I wouldn't speak to anyone for so long that I began to think it was impossible for anyone to love me. That maybe I am the problem… but then I went to Shadowborn Academy. A school full of kids like me that have never been loved, and they showed me how to embrace that. Being loved is nothing until you learn loving yourself is everything. Is that 'tell me your truth' enough?"

He looks over his shoulder and smiles. "You are wiser than you look."

"Not just a pretty face." I snort, then arch a brow at him. "Your turn."

His voice is gravelling, almost lost. "A lie ruined my life but if I could do it all over again, I would. Lying that one time saved someone I loved but it cost me."

"Cost you what?" When he doesn't answer, I add with a smirk, "You're a peculiar guy, Alex."

I slide past him, my boots sinking into the snow. He still doesn't say anything, but I feel his eyes on me all the way through the forest and to the bottom of the mountain. It takes forever to reach the bottom. My legs ache and I feel tired down to the bone, but I won't give up. You'd think our kit would've had some water.

The dark clouds eventually give way and it starts to heavy snow. My lashes are flecked with snowdrops, and I realise that being out in the open isn't the best idea in weather like this. The clouds are too thick anyway and the wind is picking up. We need to find shelter and figure out where we should go next.

"There's a cave over there. Maybe it could be another way down," Alex shouts over the wind, stretching his long arm in one direction. I just manage to see a small black cave in the distance. I don't think you would know it's there unless you look right at it. "It's too fucking cold to stay out here. Freezing to death is pointless."

"You're right. We should go to the cave," I agree, hoping we can find something better in there.

"Watch out!"

I barely register his words when I'm tackled off my feet. The air is kicked from my lungs with the impact and I land on my side, half-submerged in the snow. I roll over and grab my daggers on instinct, but the crushing weight that steps on my foot has me screaming into the blizzard. With all the snowdrops collecting on my lashes, I struggle to see it.

But then I can hear it—the powerful roar of an enormous beast.

"Izora!"

The fear in Alex's voice is palpable, mirroring exactly how I feel inside. Shaking, I thrust my dagger out like a shield, hoping to catch what I can only assume is a polar bear. The beast lifts its paw and swipes the air. Alex darts effortlessly, just managing to avoid its claws by a hair. I scramble to the side and onto my feet, taking up the rear in an effort to help him. My breathing has become laboured, each breath I drag in like ice clawing at my lungs. I know I need to act fast. This bear might only be a simulation, but we can still die in this game. It'd be game over for the both of us.

I move to the side, aiming my knife at the bear's stomach. It's impossible to get a clean shot with all the snow. Fuck!

"Alex?" I call out, hoping he's still alive. I may not trust him, but there is safety to be found in numbers, just like right now.

I can't see Alex with all the snow. I can only hear the bear roaring. I wipe my face and search through the snow the best I can. A blurry figure moves around the bear, and I know it's Alex. At least he's still alive. Gripping my dagger tighter, I go to attack the bear's vulnerable side, but then it lets out a piercing roar before collapsing into the snow. Its blood oozes out from its skull, where Alex has thrust a machete, pinning it to the snow. As quickly as the polar bear died, it erupts into dust just like the tiger did.

"Did that... did that really just fucking happen?" I pant, staring in awe at where the beast had laid just seconds ago.

Alex picks his knife up and wipes the blood off in the snow. "Yeah, it happened. Let's get going before any more nasty surprises jump out at us."

Even with the wind and snow, I can hear how calm he is. How can he be so calm in this situation? Fake bear or not, that was freaking intense. He turns toward the cave and I follow him, hoping we don't find another animal wanting to kill us.

By the time we reach the cave, the snow is so heavy that I can barely feel my fingers. We both run inside and pause to shake all the snow off. I grip my pickaxe tightly in my numb hand and look around the deep cave riddled in dampness. There is a dim light shining from the depths but it's silent, so I doubt there is a creature in here.

Only one way to find out.

I freeze as Alex steps closer and lifts his hand, placing it on my cheek. For a second there's a buzz from his touch that I can't explain, and instantly I feel like I don't want him to let go.

"If you think you have a chance of sleeping with me, think again," I warn, narrowing my eyes into slits. "I don't like an audience or fucking strangers."

But he doesn't move his hand away as he closes his eyes. Umm. Okay, maybe this guy is crazier than I thought.

His lips twitch in amusement before he starts softly saying words I don't recognise or understand. Slowly, a hot glow spreads from my cheek and rapidly fills my body, making me feel warm. I lift my hand to see my skin is glowing with a soft blue hue.

"Light magic. How the fuck can you do that?" I demand, stepping away from him. He doesn't explain himself as he starts to glow the same as me, and he heads into the cave. Gritting my teeth, I jog to catch up to him and swing my pickaxe under his neck once more. "Tell me how!"

"I won't answer you if any answer I give is going to be a lie," he calmly replies, like he doesn't have something sharp pressed against his neck; like I'm a normal girl and not an inmate who is accused of killing five men.

At this point, I don't know which of us is crazy.

"Then don't lie!"

He shakes his head, the blade sliding against his skin. "Kill me because this is an answer you cannot have," he taunts, and I all but growl as I lower my pickaxe.

Crazy bastard. He must want me to kill him.

"If your answer puts my life in danger at any point, I'm going to chop off your precious jewels first," I counter and swiftly turn around, heading into the cave with his laughter following me.

The cavern gets bigger the more we walk into it until we reach the middle, or near enough, and see where the light is coming from. The centre of the mountain is a long open pillar of ice, stretching from the tip of the mountain and right down to the bottom I suspect. Light bounces off the ice, illuminating every inch of the cave, but it's still pretty dark in places. The ice is harsh, jagged in many places and I wonder if at one point this was a waterfall. I inch closer to the edge, looking down and seeing the ropes

122

on the other side. There must have been a bridge at some point as two long ropes hang down the ice. It's weirdly mesmerising.

"We should see how long the rope is and head down. The pickaxes will help us get through the ice there," he suggests like the threat of me killing him is completely forgotten.

"It's too dangerous," I reply.

"And the only way. We will die in the snowstorm." He states, heading around the ice. Kneeling on the edge, he starts pulling on the rope.

"Any chance you can shift into a bird and fly down?" I kneel next to him, piling up the other rope as we need to check them both.

"I don't shift into a bird, wolf," he grunts as he yanks up the rope, making a small pile.

"How do you know I prefer my wolf?"

"You have wolf eyes," he counters with a cheeky grin.

This guy.

We figure out the rope is pretty long and it should get us to the end. If not, we have knives to dig into the ice and climb down the rest of the way. The pickaxe should help with any other ice we get stuck with. Alex chucks the ropes down, and I slide the pickaxe into my belt of knives, leaving my spare dagger behind since my belt is full. I wrap the rope around my waist and hold on as I edge myself over. Alex is quicker at climbing but it takes me a while. I'm at least thankful for the magic glow that gives me a good idea of where I'm going. How did he manage to do that?

About half an hour later, my legs and arms are burning and shaking from the effort. My hands are covered in cuts from digging into the rope. Every step down is painful, but I swallow any cries of protests that threaten to leave my lips.

"Watch out!" Alex shouts.

I swing the rope to the side just in time to miss a flying sword that strikes the ice, smacking into it and the sound rings through my ears as I turn around. Just under us is a clearing, much like the one above, and just our luck, four wolves circle the pillar we are in. The alpha, Coen, isn't shifted. He just stands with knives in his hand and a smirk on his face. The wolves growl and snap at the rope below us and I know if we go past them, we're dead.

If we fall, we're dead.

And if Coen starts throwing knives, we're defenseless and quite possibly fucked.

Just as I think it, Coen throws a knife and it misses my leg by a hair. His smug laugh rings through the mountain. I turn to see Alex placing his hands on the ice and closing his eyes.

"Fall when I tell you, and I promise to catch you," he orders as another knife slams into the ice by my hand.

I swallow hard. That was way too close for comfort. A few inches to the left and he would have gotten me. Alex's hands are glowing red, getting brighter and brighter by the second until the magic spreads through the ice like a virus. It shoots across the pillar, casting a crimson glow onto the alpha and wolves below.

"Let go!"

The second Alex says it, I release the rope and let myself fall. Alex jumps off and he almost floats for a moment as the ice around him shatters. The wolves try to scamper away, but the ice plunges through them, spraying their blood and guts everywhere like a crushed watermelon. As I almost plummet to my own death, somehow I know that Alex will catch me. And he does. His arms are around me in an instant, and he's pulling the rope out of nowhere and swinging us into a clearing.

We both roll onto the rough ground, somehow with me ending up on top of him. I duck my head into his chest as the ice pillar collapses inwards with a crash and the cave plunges into darkness. Both of our glowing bodies cast a bright sapphire hue around us and his are watching me so closely. I can feel his hands resting on my hips and his hot, rapid breathing fanning my face. His grip on me feels like he's protecting me like some helpless damsel in distress.

Something I've never been, and will never be.

"Thank you," I say, scrambling off him and standing up.

I reach for my belt of knives on instinct, swearing under my breath when I realise it must have fallen off. Where the heck could it have landed? Alex slides a dagger out of his own holster and hands it to me. Gods, the number of times he's saved my life or made me owe him something is adding up by the minute, and I don't like it. I don't like owing anyone debts in the first place. I take the dagger without another word, knowing I need to defend myself.

"I saw an exit over there," Alex states, gesturing somewhere in the darkness.

I go to follow when I see something in the ice that fell. I walk closer to the edge and look down to where the bottom of the pillar smashed in a circle. Right in the middle is a small, purple icebox that glows like we do.

That's it.

I glance up to see Alex's eyes intent on the prize too, and he looks up, smirking once more before he pounces.

No chance, dickhead!

I run and jump after him, throwing myself on his back while he reaches for the box. He grunts as I knock him to the ground and aim my knife at his shoulder. He grabs my arm, twisting it behind my back until I drop the knife. I let out a hiss, pain stabbing through me, before he can get any leverage, I lift my other hand and punch him hard in his face. He laughs and he shoves me to the side and uses his weight to pin me down. I kick and flail beneath him, but he's too heavy. He leans down closer, his breath tickling my ear, and I crane my neck to glare at him, witnessing the smirk of short-lived triumph on his face. If he thinks he won this round, he doesn't know me.

I'm Izora Dawn and I never let a guy get one over on me.

As he twists me around so that I'm facing him, I grab a shard of ice lying nearby, and I slam it into his chest, sliding through his lower ribs if I place it right. The pain distracts him and he gasps, blood surfacing around the tip of the ice. I knee him hard in his stomach and push him off me and crawl my way to the box.

So close, so... close...

The second I touch the box, a bright purple light burns my eyes and I scream, letting go. Shadows dance against my lids, and when I open them again, I'm on the floor in a dark, warm room. But I'm not alone. I shoot onto my feet as Alex stares down at me, his arms crossed and his injury... just gone. In fact, his clothes are different now and familiar. The dark trousers, the crisp white shirt...the gold pin. As I search his face, his features morph as the magic wears off, and in its place is the puppetmaster of Shadowborn Prison.

Governor Gold.

Dark black paint is drawn in a line across his eyes, covering the face tattoos and making his golden eyes seem that much...more. His wavy brown hair falls over his forehead, the locks look soft and my hands itch to run my fingers through them. Or grab them and slam his head into the nearest wall. I'm not sure yet.

"Congratulations on beating me and earning my orb, as well as winning this week's Blood Trials. I'm Zavier Alexander Gold and you've gained two rewards. One is from me, so make it worth it when you ask for them now."

"You lied," I growl, the relief of the Blood Trials being over sinking in. "So much for hating lies!"

His lips tilt up in amusement, and I suspect he wants to laugh. "I never lied once."

I glare at him, still trying to catch my breath. "Where have you taken me?"

"To the winner's room within the auditorium. Here, you get to pick your prizes."

I'm still trying to wrap my head around what just happened. Alex, who was actually Gold pretending to be a player, saved my life, then tried to take it, and now he's saying I won this weekend's Blood Trials? That would mean... I impressed him. Time for my next move.

"I want a room, a decent room. In fact, one of the best ones here," I say, brushing the melting snow off my clothes.

Gold inclines his head. "You can have room 2300 which is on the same floor as me. Only the best."

I'm surprised at the choice of rooms but this only puts my plan further into action.

I'm going to be the best fucking neighbour he has ever had.

We both watch each other for a long moment as I think about what I want next. I never planned for a second reward. I can't ask him to get me out of here, not when there must be people watching, so I have to be smart.

I need to win his heart and there isn't a good way of doing that when he's so cold and distant.

"I want you to teach me light magic spells once I'm released from here."

Another curt nod from him. "Deal."

He walks away as the darkness in the room fades and is replaced with cheering inmates.

I won.

Just like I told him I would.

CHAPTER TWELVE

Izora

AXEL WRAPS HIS STRONG ARMS AROUND ME AND crushes my face to his chest. "Praise the fucking gods you made it!"

I pat him on the back, muffling, "Thanks, Axel, but... can't breathe..."

"Easy up there," Memphis tells him, pulling me from Axel's suffocating embrace. "You fought well, kid. There's not a person in this room who'd wanna get on your bad side now. Not that we'd let them."

He points to the enormous screens hanging from the ceiling. They're each displaying various scenes from my time in the arena; the tiger and polar bear; watching the guys get eaten by the monster eels; climbing the frozen waterfall with Alex aka Gold; fighting with him over the box at the end.

Winning.

Everyone is cheering and watching them like it's their victory as well as mine.

This entire system is so fucked up.

And I desperately need a shower. I wonder if my new room will have a bath? I took that for granted back home. Now I really miss it.

"You're still shaking," Axel comments, eyeing me closely. "Must be the adrenaline. Let's get you to your new room before you crash."

I nod, following them out of the room, which is difficult with everyone congratulating me.

"About time those fuckin' mutts died," someone shouts, receiving a loud cheer.

"Wonder who the next pack'll be…"

I wonder, too. There were still only five wolves in the arena with me, which means Tyler never participated. I highly doubt I've seen the last of him. I push those thoughts from my mind, focusing on my prize. Not only did I get a new room, but I'm going to be on the same floor as the governor. If that doesn't scream 'getting close', I don't know what will. It's definitely setting the wheels into motion.

Outside the room, Luke is waiting for me. A sour-face woman stands beside him, dressed in a coral nurse uniform, and she doesn't look pleased to see that I won.

"Once you are changed, you'll come to the infirmary," she orders, pivoting on her heel and marching up the stairs.

"What for?" I ask Luke, because clearly, the nurse isn't going to answer me.

"Just a quick medical check," he answers.

Axel wraps an arm around my shoulders. "Well, I'll go with her then since that cow isn't waiting."

"You're not her warden," Luke growls, swatting his hand away and ushering me up the steps.

I glance back at them, mouthing, "See you later", to which they both reply with a salute and head back into the room. Meanwhile, Luke escorts me to the locker room, and I change into my clothes. He then takes me up to the infirmary in the east wing of the prison. I remember this place now just from the antiseptic smell. He took me through here on the way to the morgue.

The nurse who I saw just moments ago leads me to a spare bed and pulls the curtain around. Snapping on a pair of latex gloves, she begins her check-up while Luke waits by the curtain.

The examination is surprisingly quick and not too invasive. Apparently, they just want to check I don't have any broken bones—you know, like they actually give a fuck. I'm administered some pain killers and told by the nurse that I can go. Or at least, I'm almost sent on my way. The curtain is yanked open and a male in a lab coat steps forward.

"Izora Dawn?"

I throw my legs over the bed, slipping my feet into my trainers. "I thought I was good to go? Where's my warden?"

Luke isn't waiting for me like I thought he was.

The man's pale blue eyes flicker to the nurse and then

to me. "I'm Doctor Frank. If you come with me, we can get you tested in the lab and take it from there."

"L-lab? No, thanks. That sounds sketchy. Luke!"

He appears almost immediately, a little flushed in the face and out of breath. "Not this one, Doc. Governor's orders."

Doctor Frank and the nurse both look at each other before the doctor nods and they leave.

I push off the hospital bed and go to Luke. "What did he mean by lab? Tested for what?"

"It's nothin' you need to worry about."

By his countenance alone, I know this topic isn't up for discussion. So many questions fill my mind, but I decide to wait until a better time to voice them. I don't want to tick Luke off even more.

"Fine. Do I get to see my new room now?" I try to hide the escalating excitement in my voice, but it creeps through. "I'm dying for a shower. I stink like death."

Luke spins me around, his grip on my shoulders surprisingly tender. "I'll take you to your new place."

"If you take me to another cage," I warn, following him out of the infirmary and into a long grey corridor, "I'll be bitterly disappointed, Luke. I never fought for my life for that."

"No," he agrees, "you didn't. Follow me."

I do so all the way to the other end of the prison. Tucked in the far-left corner is the highest tower I saw on the night I arrived. We start to climb the spiral stairs, and Luke looks over his shoulder at me.

"This is where most of the staff sleep. Gold is on the top floor. Your suite is there, too."

I nearly choke on my own spit. "S-suite? Well, colour me surprised. Never thought I'd get something that nice… even though I did technically ask for the best. Will you still be my warden?"

Finally, his features soften and he smiles, just a little. "Of course."

We climb the rest of the stairs in comfortable silence, passing many doors on the way. Right at the very top, a circular window bleeds sunlight onto the floor. Luke takes a turn at the window, and we enter a dimly lit hallway. The floor is dark wood instead of tiles and the walls are papered tastefully—both a stark contrast to the rest of the prison. There's an air of intimacy up here and the soothing ambiance reminds me a little of home. I swallow the lump gathering into my throat. Now really isn't the time to get nostalgic.

"Here we are."

Luke stops outside a door with the numbers 2-3-0-0 inscribed into the rich wood. At the other end of the hall, just slightly to the left, is a room that says GOV, and my heart skips a beat. I never expected to be *that* close to him.

I hold my breath as I watch Luke slide his pass against the lock and open the door. He motions for me to enter first. I step over the threshold, releasing my breath, but it hitches when I see my new cell. Or more accurately, suite. There's nothing at all cell-like about this room other than the barred floor-to-ceiling windows and motion sensors on the door. The open concept is basic but spacious, with a huge queen bed pressed against a tall wooden headboard that stretches to the ceiling. The bed is actually on a platform, and down the two steps into the living area is a trio of leather sofas, a flat-screen tv mounted to the wall above an unlit fireplace and a huge, shaggy, white rug under the sculpted coffee table. The kitchen is near the door, a little nook with basic appliances and a breakfast table with two stools. I think I spot an ensuite door on the same level as my bedroom.

My boots slide against the shiny floorboards as I take a look around. The setting sunlight pouring through the window gleams against all of the beautiful furnishings within the room. I can't believe this is my place now. No more cage. No more springy mattress digging into my back. No more clothes dumped in a pile. I step up onto the platform and brush my fingers against the chestnut drawers and wardrobe, feeling all the soft little grooves of the intricate patterns.

Luke steps farther into the room with me, examining the interior with pinched eyes. "Is this why you did it? For all of… this?"

I turn around, frowning. "Isn't that why most of the players enter, to get nice things?"

"Yeah. I just never thought you were the materialistic type."

"And I'm not. Not really." I spread my fingers through the furry rug draped over the foot of the bed. "It's just part of my bigger plan."

"To get Gold to stop the Trials?" He shakes his head slowly, almost pitifully. "It ain't ever gonna happen."

I turn my steely eyes on him. "You have such tremendous faith in me."

"More than you know," he mutters, though I just manage to catch the words. "Things don't change now that you're up here. You might be safer in this room, but that doesn't mean you're free to do whatever you want. There are still potential inmates out to get you and I'm still your warden."

I flop down onto the bed, huffing at him. "Way to harsh my buzz."

"Just sayin' how it is. I don't pussyfoot around."

That he doesn't.

The way he says 'pussy' does serious things to me, though…things I really shouldn't be feeling.

I roll onto my stomach and look up at him through my lashes. "Are you at least happy I'm still alive, Warden? Come on, say it. Tell me you missed me."

Luke's eyebrows knit together and his lips close, then they part again. "You're a pain in the ass, jaybird, but you're my pain in the ass. My ward. And every time you walk through those damn doors, I think it's the last time I'll ever see you. What'll I do then, eh?"

A giddy feeling twirls around in my stomach. I laugh it off.

"Easy. You'd get another prisoner to take care of," I point out, pushing up onto my elbows. "One who isn't a pain in the ass."

I smile at him, and to my relief, he slowly returns it. There's still a level of reluctance that I see burning in his gaze. If he wishes to refute the matter further, he doesn't.

"I was thinking…"

"Oh, gods," he groans, and I shoot a pretend glare.

"Since I won the Blood Trials and all, and I got this fancy big room, maybe we should celebrate."

That catches his attention. "Celebrate how?" he asks curiously.

"I…" I trail off, feeling incredibly stupid. I'm not even sure how we could celebrate since we aren't allowed booze, I'm not allowed to go anywhere unescorted, and I barely have any friends to celebrate with. "Never mind. I think I'm just gonna go for a shower. Do you think I could skip the mess hall tonight?"

He nods. "I'll bring your dinner up."

I say thanks and hop off the bed, making my way into what I think is the bathroom. The room is huge with a waterfall shower, clawfoot tub, gorgeous vanity, and a three-piece suite. Sheesh. When Gold said this floor was 'only the best', he wasn't kidding. What fighting for your life can buy you. I have a feeling I'm going to be spending a lot of time in this beautiful tub.

I run the taps and strip off my clothes. Grabbing the robe hanging on the back of the door, I wrap myself in the plush material and wait for my bath to finish running. The steam from the hot water streams up, turning my face pink, but it's just the way I like it. I throw my robe off and slip into the bath, settling down with a contented sigh.

I must spend at least twenty minutes in the bath, soaking up the warmth and luxury. When I step out of the bathroom, unwrapping my hair from its towel, I find a food tray on the foot of my bed. I sink down on the soft mattress and wolf the casserole down. That's one thing that always surprises me post-Blood Trials—still having an appetite.

I glance at the digital clock on the wall. It's only gone four-thirty. Back home, that would've been a good time to hop into some fluffy pajamas. If only I had some. I tighten my bathrobe and walk over to the wardrobe, pulling the doors open. I expect to find the bland clothing I was given on day one. What I find is something completely different. There are actually colourful items of clothing hanging on the velvet hangers; pink chiffon blouses, green and blue T-shirts, navy jeans, autumnal sweaters, and various other items, including two-piece pajamas and a onesie.

All my size—all for me.

My eyes sting with tears. It's so stupid to get emotional over this. I fought hard for it, literally with my life. I don't deserve to be in this prison. But after what I've gone through, I deserve to live like a normal person again, even if that only means some new clothes.

I take my time looking through the wardrobe. Curious about the drawers, I open them all but they're mostly empty. The top one has all my belongings from the cage. I grab some fresh underwear and go back to the wardrobe, deciding to wear the woolen pink dress and skinny jeans. Actually, it's probably just a sweater, but it drowns my small-ass self. I have at least three hours of downtime before lockdown, and I'll probably leave my room soon, so I pull out a pair of soft, light navy jeans to avoid any unwanted attention. I already get enough as it is, and it's not because of my hot body. It's because they see me as a threat.

I hear the door opening and I grin. This is the kind of attention I *do* want. Instead of rushing into the bathroom to change, I untie my robe. It puddles onto the floor around my ankles and I turn around so that I'm facing Luke when he enters.

"Well, fuck, if that ain't a beautiful view…"

"A-Axel!" I grab the dress and cover my body with it, looking over at him in horror. Well, not in complete horror. It is Axel, after all, the hottest inmate in this prison.

Luke barges past him and Memphis—*oh fuck!*—and into the room, grumbling, "Any normal person would change in the bathroom!" Whipping around to face the guys, he orders, "Look the fuck away. There's nothin' to see here."

"Oh, there's plenty to see," Axel says, sweeping his lustful gaze over my body. "And Daddy likes."

Memphis rolls his eyes and spins him around. I should totally be mortified, but it's so funny that I can't help but laugh. Luke's irate expression and Axel's gooey eyes just made my week. Still giggling to myself, I bundle my clothes up and dash into the bathroom, quickly changing. I find a hairbrush on the vanity, and I drag it through my wet hair. It's annoying how the bristles always hit my collar. Opting for something different, I twist my hair into two braids. Wow, wild.

"What are you here for anyway?" I ask the guys as I step out of the bathroom.

"We came to congratulate you," Memphis says from beside the sofas.

"And I brought booze." Axel sets down a bottle of whisky and drapes an ankle over his knee, his hands clasped behind his head like he's Selena's gift to women. Wouldn't be too far off. A mischievous grin plays on his lips. "Time to celebrate, cutie."

CHAPTER THIRTEEN

Izora

I sit next to Axel on the sofa and glance nervously at Luke. "I thought you said no booze ever?"

He shrugs, walking over from the kitchen with a tray of glasses. "You won the Blood Trials. You deserve to celebrate."

Axel throws his head back and laughs, the sound deep and infectious. "Mate, she fucking *slayed* that arena. Everyone keeps banging on about it."

I beam at the compliment, feeling surprisingly relaxed after my bath. It's the most relaxed I've felt since I came here. Luke sets the tray in the middle of the coffee table and takes the bottle of whisky from Axel. He prepares a round of drinks. His knuckles are blanched and his throat keeps jerking. I don't think he's at all comfortable. Why would he put himself through this just for me?

G. BAILEY & SCARLETT SNOW

Pulling my legs up onto the sofa, I turn to Memphis. "What do you think? How'd I do?"

His mouth quirks into a lopsided smile. "You owned it, kid. Did us all proud just like me and Axe knew you would."

Luke breathes heavily through his nose, apparently not in agreement. He hands each of us a drink, and we take a moment to sip in slightly awkward silence. I think what we're missing right now is some music. Since the only person in here who can magic is Luke, I ask him.

"Music?" His forehead creases as he looks around.

"Yeah, music. We can play it quietly though so Gold doesn't hear."

Axel snorts and throws back his drink. "That Draconian can hear through every wall in this prison. Nothing gets past him."

A cold draft creeps into the room. I feel it trickle down my spine and lift the ends of my hair ever so lightly. Odd. There aren't any open doors or windows in the room. I take a huge gulp of the strong whisky, nearly finishing it, and choke at the overpowering taste. The very second I catch my breath, someone knocks on the door.

I push off the sofa, laughing. "Okay, Luke, who else did you invite? Warden Kyle?"

My stomach clenches at the prospect. *Please, Goddess, no.*

Luke manages to get some music on the tv, and I walk over to answer the door. A shudder wracks through my body when I pull it open only to find Gold standing in the doorway. It's like I felt his presence before anyone else in the room. He's no longer wearing the clothes he donned in the arena, nor the face painting. In the short time since I last saw him, he's freshened up into a sharp black suit with a blood-red tie, and he's slicked his hair back, but still a few loose strands brush against his temple.

His unusual eyes peer over my shoulder at the guys. "Ahh. I thought you were having a celebratory gathering." His gaze snaps back to meet mine. "Might I at least join in to congratulate this week's winner?"

"But, sir—I mean, Gold, you're, umm, well… the *governor!*" I blurt out, a ferocious surge of heat assaulting my cheeks. Why in the name of Selena would the governor of this hellhole want to join our party?

Gold clicks his fingers and three boxes of pizza appear in his hand.

"Come on in," I say, yanking the door open so wide I nearly break the hinges.

Gold places the boxes onto the kitchen counter, dusts his hands, and walks over to the guys. I close the door and follow him. He sits on the sofa that hasn't been claimed by any of the guys. As soon as he leans over to pour some whisky, his attention diverted, Axel mouths "What the fuck" to me.

"Governor Gold," he greets out loud, forcing a smile. "Come to join the fun?"

"No. I came to spoil it and make everything awkward as shit with my presence." He places his hands on the back of the sofa, ever so slightly lifting a brow. "You know I can sniff through walls as well as hear. Whisky's my favorite. It's Luke's, too, isn't it?"

Luke rests on the edge of Gold's sofa. "Seize the day, Gov. Ain't that what you always tell me?"

Gold chuckles, glancing at him. "Yet you rarely listen."

"Only when you're right." Luke winks and lifts his glass to the governor.

Their informal exchange is nothing that I expected. I look between the two. You'd almost think they were friends instead of what they truly are.

"I thought your name was Alex," I point out, deliberately sliding onto the sofa beside him. "Or rather, Alexander."

"I did say that."

"So you lied?" I challenge. "You said you hate lies."

"I never lied. My middle name is Alexander, first name Zavier."

I lift my legs up onto the sofa again, regretting my decision to wear jeans. I bet showing some flesh would really work in my favour right now.

"That's good to know…" Axel looks over at Memphis, who's already standing up to grab a pizza box. "Fancy a slice, Gov?"

Gold nods, and Axel settles back on the sofa. The tension between the guys is visibly suffocating. Figuring I best change the atmosphere stat, I clap my hands and stand from the sofa.

"Wait! I have a better idea. More booze, anyone?"

If in doubt, get everyone drunk ASAP.

"Fuck yeah," Axel says. "Good call, cutie."

Gold slides him a curious glance that leisurely rests on me. "Cutie?"

"What? I am cute," I say, fluttering my lashes at him. "Admit it, sir."

He scoffs and watches me pour the drinks. Memphis comes back with a pizza box and extra glass, which he hands the latter to Gold. Axel bounces off the sofa to reach for Memphis' opened pizza like it's a pot of gold, but Memphis moves his arm out of the way.

"Get your fucking own," he grumbles. "You don't get this size sharing food."

Axel mumbles something about being a tight ass and makes his way to the kitchen, probably to stake claim on an entire pizza.

"Here you go." I pass Gold his drink. "So, why are you really here?" I probe him, sinking back into the sofa.

I watch him sip his drink and swallow the contents with a sigh, his eyes dipping as if savoring the taste. You'd think he'd never tasted whisky before. Surely he can drink as much alcohol as he wants in here? He's the governor. It's only inmates that have to smuggle things like this in…

"The Gov always stops by to congratulate the winner," Luke explains, throwing back the rest of his drink. I hear it gulp down his throat. "Usually he's the one who brings the booze."

"And usually you're the one who drinks most of it," Gold chides, shaking his head. He waves his hand and three bottles of wine appear on the table, complete with five crystal glasses. "In ancient times, the king or queen would have given the winners a necklace with the Star of Luna on it. It was their reward for becoming their warrior. Now I don't have any of those, but I do have wine that gets shipped to me from King Cyrus. It always goes down well with the winners."

"It'll certainly go well here," Memphis comments, putting his pizza aside to crack open a bottle. "Do you drink wine, kid?"

I nod at him, fully aware of Gold's eyes still pressed on me. "Yes. My mother was a *big* wine drinker. She insisted I become fluent in it when I turned sixteen."

To my surprise, they each laugh at my joke. The alcohol must be kicking in because they start to chat amongst themselves, which is a major relief. I thought this whole night was ruined when the governor walked through the door. Now I'm beginning to think I might actually be able to kill three birds with one stone here. I have Luke, Axel, and Gold at my side. If I could get them to let their guards down, who knows what will happen?

I pretty much have Luke's attention already, but I need to be careful not to lose it. He has a tendency to get jealous at times. I don't understand why. I mean, there's plenty of me to go around. Gotta admit though—seeing a guy's protective side is a huge turn on for me. Jealousy, not so much, but that 'I'm claiming her, too' protectiveness? I'm so down for that, and I totally get those vibes from Luke. I just don't think he's ever managed to differentiate between feeling protective and jealous. Note to self: *Must help the sexy warden fix that.*

I've also seen the way Axel looks at me. He's not so much jealous as he is eager to rip my clothes off and fuck me against the wall. He's actually the one I relate to the most so far in this prison. I feel so safe in his company. He's the loveable, big giant who I bet isn't afraid to spank a bitch when she's been naughty. Oh, I really hope I'm right about him. I think he could be some fun while I'm incarcerated here.

And then there's Zavier Gold, the governor of Shadowborn Prison. Everything about him should send me running for the hills. I should hate him and want nothing to do with him. The only thing I *should* want to see is his corpse rotting in the ground. And yet, right now, right here, I want him to kiss me. I want to feel his hands threading in my hair and his lips against my mouth.

How can I be thinking like this?

He's the one who created and clearly loves the Blood Trials. It's just an ancient tradition to him and the fae. It's suicide for most of the inmates and luxuries for the winners. The winners who he then takes wine to for putting on a grand display and not being slaughtered.

That's fucked up.

What's more fucked up is that his presence doesn't repulse me as much as it should.

I frown into my glass, swirling the remains of the alcohol around. I know Professor Mune would tell me how all great people need to make great sacrifices to achieve the greater good. Is sacrificing my moral compass great enough? What if I need to sacrifice more? What if...

what if I need to give these men my heart just to get my freedom?

"A kid like you shouldn't be frowning."

I flinch out of my reverie and look up at Memphis who's holding out his hand.

"I'm no good at dancing, kid, but I'd rather make a twat of myself than see you look sad."

He doesn't have to tell me twice. I swallow the last of my drink and take his hand. He lifts me effortlessly onto my feet. The music is rock with light jazz undertones, yet Memphis twirls me under his arm like we're at a fancy ball. Maybe it's all the twirling, but the whisky has started to hit me, and I laugh, completely forgetting about my worries from before. I'm glad Memphis only wants to be my friend. That'll give my poor heart a much-needed reprieve. Plus, I get my silver-fox fill with Professor Mune. He's someone I've had my eye on for months, and I don't plan on giving up anytime soon.

The music shifts into edgier beats, and Memphis lets me go to refill our glasses, this time with wine. I'm all happy now and carefree—exactly what I've been itching for since this entire nightmare began. As soon as I throw back the wine, Axel takes my hand and spins me around into his arms. He brings our bodies closer, so close that our hips press together and his hand lands on my ass. He gives a firm squeeze that makes me squeal in delight.

I move my body to the music, sliding Luke a veiled glance to gauge his reaction. He's too busy drinking and talking to the Memphis to notice we're breaking prison rules. But the governor is watching us dance, his entire expression wiped clean of emotion, apart from his eyes. I know what burns within them.

Lust.

Desire.

Want.

I twist in Axel's arms, pressing my ass against his hardened cock. I hear him growl in my ear and grab my hair, forcing my head back as we grind to the beat. All the while, I look into Gold's eyes, my gaze never once moving from his. Slowly, the corners of his mouth upturn into a grin, and I know I've finally got his attention.

The song changes. Axel spins me around so that I'm facing him again, bringing our noses inches from each other.

"I want you, Izora," he tells me, loud enough for only me to hear over the music. "I want every fucking inch of you."

I grin, sliding my palm down his muscular chest. "I know you do."

My fingers just reach the band of his jeans when a hand that is definitely not Axel's clamps on my shoulder. Luke rips me from Axel's grip and drags me back.

"No touchin'—"

"—other inmates," I finish off for him, groaning like some petulant child. He's such a total buzzkill. "I'm sorry. But look at that handsome beast. Can you really blame me?"

The guys laugh, and even Gold smirks.

"Stand down, Luke," he orders, then turning to me, warns, "Behave, Izora. Don't make me regret bringing you wine. Winner or not, you must abide by prison rules."

As if you weren't enjoying it.

I seize an unopened bottle and hug it to my chest. "Don't take it anyway! Not the wine—anything but the wine!"

Goddess, I really am fucking drunk. There's no way I'd act like this otherwise.

But that's the thing.

I *miss* drinking and partying and feeling like a normal soon to be twenty-year-old. It's crazy how much you miss things once they're gone. Or doing things once your freedom has been taken from you.

"I'll be back in a moment," I say, blinking my tears away before anyone catches on. I forgot I get emotional when I'm drunk.

I rush into the bathroom and lean against the closed door. I thought having some alcohol would help me relax, not make me a total weak ass. Yeah, my life has been destroyed. I have no home, family, or friends once I get out of here. That doesn't mean I have nothing. There are people in this forest who built more from less. Things will be different in the mortal world, sure. I won't have Axel or Memphis in my life, or even Luke or Gold. But I'll have my magic—something the wardens can't take from me unless they bury me six feet under.

All I need is my powers. With them, I can clear my name from outside the forest, and avenge those who wronged me. I will do it. It's only a matter of time. The best part of all? The wardens can't stop me because, in the human world, their rules no longer apply. I can fight them back, and this time I'll have nothing to lose.

"Izora?" Luke says through the door, knocking twice. I barely step back and open my mouth when he pushes into the room. He sweeps his gaze over my body, pausing on my face. "Have you been crying?"

"I don't cry," I snap back, grimacing at him. "I'm not weak."

Slowly, he reaches out to lifts my chin and inspects me closer. "No, you're not weak. Never have been. But there ain't no shame in cryin.'"

His thumb slides along my jaw, and my pulse spikes, fluttering under the of his finger that rests on my throat. A light blush has snuck into his cheeks and his pupils are blown, intent on my lips. Tightening his grip on my face, he dents my cheek a little, and I realise that he must be drunk. He'd never touch me like this sober. He has wanted to but he always held back. His fingers slide down my throat and to the back of my neck. In one swift pull, his lips are against mine, and he's kissing me with such wild abandon that I can scarcely draw breath.

He lets go of my neck only to seize my legs and wrap them around his waist. Placing me on top of the vanity, I lace my fingers through his hair, dragging him closer, needing him more, like nothing I ever imagined.

"Oi! I need to take a slash," Axel shouts, banging on the door.

Ugh. Now that is a total mood kill.

Luke groans against my mouth, then releases me and sets me on the floor.

"That was unexpected," I whisper with a grin. "In a good way," I quickly add, seeing the troubled look on his face.

"What the fuck am I doing?" He whispers the words, too, but I don't think he intended me to hear.

Axel bangs again, jolting the door in its hinges. "I'm choking on a piss out here!"

Yanking the door open, Luke storms out of the bathroom and Axel gives a long, drawn-out whistle.

"I interrupted your freaky-freaky time, huh?"

I throw him a mock glare. "Just a bit. The bathroom is all yours."

"Thanks, cutie. Now when I get outta here, your ass is mine and we're gonna dance until curfew, ya hear?"

"You know where to find me," I slide past him, grinning. "By the pizza."

CHAPTER FOURTEEN

Izora

"YOU SEEM STRESSED TODAY, SCOTT," I comment, watching my teacher harshly scribble in his notepad.

Our private lessons have become my only constant in prison since I won the Blood Trials three weeks ago. Of course, there have been more winners since then but none have moved up to the top floor. While my room is amazing, my plan of getting closer to Gold hasn't worked so far because he's never in the damn room. I'm certain the fae doesn't sleep at all at this point. I haven't even told Scott that I entered the Blood Trials yet in fear of his reaction. He talks about them just like I had done—appalled, sickened, and completely angered by their existence. I've bitten my tongue whenever the subject has arisen, but today he appears visibly distressed, and I wonder if he's found out I participated...and that I killed someone.

"The academy..." he pauses, looking up at me. Realisation dawns on his face like he's just remembered who he's talking to or something. "It's nothing. Just your friend Corvina Charles is causing havoc."

"Isn't she always?" I say around a laugh, though it's a pained sound as I'm reminded that I'll never see Corvina or the academy or anyone outside of here for years. A nice room can't make up for the fact that it's a prison and I'm stuck here, living a shadow of a life for years.

Years...

A pang of longing for the academy and my friends, my life before all this mess, hits me hard. Tears collect on my lashes despite my best efforts and drop onto the desk, smudging my writing. Suddenly, I no longer want to learn about the *History of Magics*. My tears keep flowing and a quiver catches my lip, seconds from bursting into sobs.

"Izy?"

I glance over at my professor, my only real friend who now stands over my desk. Without a word, he lifts me out of the seat and into his arms. I press my head into his neck as he walks us back to his seat and I just cry. I've held in all the tears for my past, for Abbie's death, for everything this place has taken from me.

And will continue to take no matter what I do.

"Forgive me. I'm an asshole," Scott mutters, his lips beneath his silver beard sliding into a frown. "I'm complaining about my problems to someone locked up for something they didn't do. How inconsiderate of me."

"It's not your fault I'm—I'm in here, Scott," I say between stuttering breaths.

"Then whose fault is it?" he grumbles, placing me into his big comfy chair. He kneels down and holds my arms. "I want to break their face. I *will* break their face. Tell me who?"

The sincerity lacing his words takes me by surprise, turning my cries into a fit of giggling hysteria. My sobs still wrack through, but slowly they die into a lump in my throat that I swallow down, then wipe my eyes with my sleeve. Scott catches a solitary tear on the bottom of my chin with his thumb and smiles. It's a heartbreakingly sexy smile that makes me forget he's a little older than me, and my teacher. I only see a handsome man who could be anywhere else…but he's here, comforting me, his hand gently rubbing my arm. Gratitude surges through me. I can't bear to keep my secret anymore.

"I entered the Blood Trials and won."

The words escape my lips without me really thinking them through.

The playful expression on his face swiftly drops into one of pure anger. If he were a druid, I imagine a tornado exploding from him, sucking me in and destroying everything in its path.

"Why the fuck would you risk your life like that?" he all but roars, gripping my arm tightly, his other falling to my waist. "I came here for you. I want to protect *you*, and I will get you out of here, but I can't do any of that if you run into danger when I'm not here!"

"You don't understand…"

"I understand plenty. I've lost friends, colleagues, students…family in that arena. Why would you make me lose you, too?"

This was a really bad idea. It's also how I figured he'd react. Urgh. Why can't I keep my big mouth shut? I shrug his hands away and push off the chair. I almost reach the door when I'm filled with a surge of fury. First of all, Scott doesn't have any right to judge or put that kind of guilt on me. Second, he pretty much ignored me at the academy whenever I tried to get his attention. Even when I stayed behind class or arrived early just to get to know him, he dismissed me. Now he's here acting like I've betrayed him somehow?

I spin around, placing my hands on my hips. "Why do you only care now?"

"You want to know the reason why?" He pounces off his chair and storms over. In seconds, he has me gripped in his arms and he's pushing me up against the blackboard, his face only inches from mine. "When I first saw you in my class, I was your fucking teacher. I couldn't be more than that. I would never risk your position at the academy or my job, but I also couldn't stop thinking about you! Your beautiful silver hair, your haunting grey eyes, your perfect body that puts all fae in existence to shame… Don't you see? This is all wrong, and yet I want you, Izora. I've wanted you since the moment you first opened those pretty little lips and nothing but sarcasm came out. You made every lesson torture and I often prayed to the gods for forgiveness. I even prayed that the academy's rules would change despite reality...despite me being older. That's another reason why I stayed away. You're barely twenty and I'm thirty-four. I convinced myself you wouldn't be interested in me even if I did make a move."

"I—"

"So that's my reason. That's why I'm here and so fucking pissed that I could have lost you before I even got to know you."

He stares down at me, now waiting for my response. I don't know what words to use to explain how... happy he's just made me. My crush on him wasn't one-sided. It wasn't just me all along. He reciprocated my feelings, however he had no choice but to hold back.

I suddenly become aware of how his hard, extremely hard body is pressed into mine. I can feel his hot breath on my cheeks, and I can almost taste it; a mixture of something sweet and minty. His natural scent is alluring as much as it relaxes me, and soon I realise there is only one way I want to answer him.

Moving my head just that little bit closer, I close the space and claim his lips with my own. The first kiss is soft as we gently explore each other's mouths. But as tenderly as the kiss began, the burning desire percolating between us erupts, like a gorging fire fanning to life at long last. His hand roughly grips my hair as he deepens the kiss, pushing his hard cock into my thigh with every single movement. It's intoxicating and I moan against his mouth. Before things can go any further, he breaks away from me, as breathless as I am.

As confused about where we go from here.

I sigh a protest as he sets me down on the floor. "Let's start over again?" he suggests with a cheeky grin. "We can pretend we just met randomly and that we aren't in a prison. Tell me some things about you."

I nod, dragging my swollen bottom lip between my teeth. His eyes trace the movement. "I'm Izora Dawn and you're a damn good kisser. I used to love horse riding, my favourite colour is silver and my favourite food is pizza with pineapple, kale, and ham. Don't judge me. Oh, and I have a major fear of water."

Scott chuckles. "I'm afraid we can no longer be friends. The pizza was a deal-breaker and I am heavily judging you."

I can't help but laugh with him and gently shove his shoulder. He offers me a hand to shake which I gladly accept.

"My name is Scott Mune. I'm a professor at Shadowborn Academy and I work part-time elsewhere. I love to hunt and fish, my favourite colour is dark green and my favourite food is curry, especially the spicy kind, which is the way my mother used to make it."

"Can you cook?" I ask with interest.

"Yes, and if they ever allow me, I will bring in some food for you."

My grin stretches into a full-blood smile that hurts my cheeks. "I'd like that. The food here isn't great."

"Now tell me something else," he asks, waving a hand towards the chairs.

We sit down and for the next few hours we talk about our childhoods, our old homes and somewhat about our families. If anything, I know Professor Scott Mune a lot more by the end, and I like him a lot more, too.

Selena, help my heart, it's lost to my professor.

Stretching my arms over my head, the cold evening air blows against my bare stomach and legs. The tiny shorts and crop top likely weren't the best idea of workout clothes to wear outside tonight, but they are better than half the things I found in my new room. A light sheen of sweat covers my skin thanks to the ten laps around the prison and the thirty sit-ups I've just done. I eye the empty workout class, knowing I should go inside soon as the skies above us are looking dark and dismal, and there's a scent of rain lingering in the air. I turn around and come face to face with Luke. His blue eyes are darker than usual and his whole demeanour screams pissed off. I wonder if Axel has been talking to him today. Axel seems to piss Luke off just by breathing.

I stand completely still as he leans closer to me.

"You smell like your professor. Maybe I should attend your classes from now on?"

"I'd rather you didn't," I counter sweetly and he

163

growls. I jump out of his way when he tries to grab my arm and I grin. "Catch me if you want, warden."

I turn around and start running the empty track as fast as I can. For a moment, I think he might have given up, but then he appears in a cloud of shadows in front of me and I slam into his chest. We both get knocked to the ground, and he laughs as he rolls us over, hovering his body over mine.

"Caught you," he says with a slow chuckle, his face inches from mine.

Trying not to notice how his body feels against me, I stare up at the night sky. "You cheated."

"Look at me, not the sky," he orders. I nearly jump from his strict command. I drift my gaze back to Luke, and I don't know why I bothered looking away. His eyes are more beautiful and enchanting than the sky. "I don't think your classes with the professor are good for you."

"Only because you're jealous and strangely possessive of me," I point out and he tenses up.

"I'm lookin' out for you," he grits.

I chuckle, shaking my head. "Lie to yourself all you want."

"Tell me to leave you the fuck alone," Luke whispers, his voice full of longing and thick with desire. "Tell me to go, tell me you don't want me. Tell me anythin' that will make this easier."

"If I said any of those, it would be a lie," I answer, and we both just stare at each other for a long moment.

"Then don't complain when I never let you go, *my*

Jailbird," he softly says before pushing off me and to his feet in one go. He offers me a hand and helps me stand. Everything feels different between us now. I have the feeling I've just opened a jar I'm never going to want to re-close or cover-up. "Now get runnin.'"

I nod, moving my ass quickly out of the way as my thoughts swirl around in my head.

One thought sticks the most, though. Who knew falling for someone in prison would be so fun?

CHAPTER FIFTEEN

Izora

A S SOON AS I ENTER THE TRAINING ROOM, I SEE
him. It's like Coen's presence clawed its way to
me like a septic perfume. I still can't believe he
never died when the ice crushed him a few weeks ago.
His whole pack survived. My week was going really
well, considering, until I found out about Coen and then
yesterday happened. Somehow, every single player in the
Blood Trials died and all of them in the same way at the
same time. I knew Coen had been watching me train half
the people that went into the arena and now his cocky
grin? No, something is up, and I bet I know what.

"*You!*"

It's all I can get out as my body floods with anger.
A dark veil drops over my gaze, and all I can see is red.
I'm marching over to him with my fist raised before he
can so much as blink, and I throw the hardest punch

I'm capable of. It lands right on his mouth, knocking him off balance, but it doesn't knock him out like I was hoping. The blood that filters through his teeth is at least a bit satisfying.

Coen regains his balance and touches the edge of his lip, staining the tip of his finger with blood. Tyler dumps down his weights on the floor and storms over. I snap my head towards him, just praying he'll lay a hand on me. It'll be the last thing he ever fucking does.

"Stand back," Coen orders, lifting his hand to Tyler, who reluctantly comes to a sharp halt, his glare latched on me. "Good to see you too, Izora."

"Fuck. You."

He spits blood on the floor, his swollen lips half-tilting into an amused smile. A malicious glint flashes in his unnerving eyes. I hold his gaze though, my chest rising and falling with rapid, enraged breaths.

"What the fuck are you doing here?" I demand before he can utter a word, steeling myself to fight again. I'm so worked up I don't notice Axel coming to my side. I thought I'd escaped Luke and all the others.

"She asked you a question, Coen. Answer it," he warns, crossing his arms.

Coen just laughs. He throws his head back and laughs like this is the funniest thing in the fucking world. Gods, I want to break his neck, right here and now. But I need to know how he did it.

"Did you use magic? Drink a potion? You must've done something because none of the other players came back," I point out, my heart clenching at the thought of all the other magics that died and never came back.

"Last I checked, I'm still collared like the rest of you sorry bastards." Coen sniffs, wiping his mouth with the bottom of his tee-shirt. "Magic and potions can't cheat death."

I look him up and down with a dispassionate glare. "You're lying. Tell me how you fucking survived that arena while everyone else didn't."

Before I can get my answer, a deafening alarm sounds overhead. The doors thrust open and a swarm of wardens rush into the room, their weapons raised, yelling commands and pinning everyone down. At first, I think it's because of me, but when a warden tasers Coen to the floor I realise something entirely different is going on here.

Panic climbs into my body, replacing the anger I was nursing before.

"Ax—"

I barely get the words out when I'm seized and pushed against the nearest wall, my arms twisted behind my back. I crane my neck as much as I can and try to assess what the hell is going on here. Inmates are being held down at gunpoint, people are shouting over the siren, some inmates are resisting but it only results in them being tasered or tackled to the ground.

"We know it was you!"

Axel is shoved into the wall beside me, his cheek crushed against the cement. The two wardens pinning him down aren't being as gentle as mine. Still, Axel flashes me a grin.

"I didn't do shit," he spits back, winking at me.

The guard points his taser and sets the thing off. "Yeah, so you fucking didn't."

Axel clenches his eyes and grinds his teeth against the pain. Just watching this is unbearable.

"Please, stop it," I beg them.

"Stay down," the guard restraining me orders, pushing me harder into the wall.

"Get your fucking hands off my ward!"

My heart soars at the sound of Luke's voice. The hands holding me let go only to be replaced by Luke's.

"Hurry," he says, dragging me from the room.

"Luke, what's going on?"

He doesn't answer immediately, too focused on marching me to safety. Everywhere we go, lights flash, the siren booms and inmates are being restrained left, right, and centre. It's terrifying to be in the middle of the riot, especially when one inmate comes straight for me and Luke has to tase him to the ground. He paves the rest of the way, holding his gun out while also clenching my hand. When we reach my room, he's quick to lock us inside. Barriers that I never knew existed drop down across the door to provide additional security. My chest is rising and falling with each rapid breath as I try to make sense of what's going on.

Luke pauses at the door, his entire body locked up with a trembling rage that radiates from him. He storms over to the kitchen, opens the fridge and pulls out two bottles of water. Throwing me one, he practically devours his whole bottle, gasping for air at the end. I sit on the edge of my bed and wait until he's calmed down.

At last, he turns to me. "You okay?"

I nod, admittedly shocked by the whole ordeal. "I've never been part of a riot before. That's what it was, right? A prison riot?"

"Yeah."

"Is Axel and the others going to be okay?"

He gives a grim nod. "Yeah."

Another one-word answer. I think he's still too heated to talk. Maybe he needs a different topic until I'm sure he's settled.

"What made you want to become a warden here?" I probe him, patting the space beside me on the bed.

Luke hesitates, glancing at the door and back again. "My sister was a prison warden and so was my father before they died," he answers, walking over and sitting on the bed. "My uncle still works here."

I can sense his magic simmering in his body, the familiar burning leaves smell invading my nostrils. That tells me he is *really* pissed. I wonder what set him and the riot off.

"So this job runs in the family, huh?" I think about the last part. "Who is your uncle?"

He casts me a guarded glance, then looks back at the door, his grip tightening on his gun. "Warden Kyle."

"No. Fucking. Way. That asshole? I mean, sorry, but… he's, uhh, intense?"

"That's one word for him."

"What happened to your sister and dad?"

Another glance, and a crease forms between his brows as he considers my question. "They were killed, by inmates, in a riot much like this. My uncle never got over it."

The silence that drifts between us should be tense, but it's not. I inch closer to him, pressing my palm into the blanket draped over my bed. Just a few more inches and I'll be able to touch his hand.

"I'm sorry about your family," I whisper, slyly touching him with my pinkie.

Luke frowns my hand, but then slowly, like sunrays breaking out through the clouds, his frown lets up.

"So you wanted to become a warden because your dad and sis were?" I repeat, hoping this subject is a good one for him. He seems to loosen up a little when he talks about his family.

"I had no choice. None of us here do," he mutters, then realising what he just said, looks up at me in alarm. "Enough questions for now, jaybird."

I nod. "Okay. Then how about we play a game?"

He quirks his mouth. "What game?"

"How long can Izora and Luke sit on this bed without kissing again."

Finally, he laughs, just a little one, and it makes me stupidly happy.

His laugh is quick to vanish when someone knocks on the door.

"It's Gold. Open up."

CHAPTER SIXTEEN

Izora

"**G**UARD THE DOOR, WARDEN." GOLD'S VOICE all but growls as he slams the door, his coat whipping around him.

Luke stands from my side and looks between us once, not moving from his spot until I nod with a small smile. He then turns on his heel and makes sure to smack his shoulder into Gold's as he passes by to stand in front of the door, his arms crossed and his eyes never leaving mine. Gold watches him with a look of murder on his face.

"Sorry about him," I say hurriedly, hoping to diffuse the tension. "He's a little moody after today."

Gold snaps his gaze to me. "He is my warden and not yours to make excuses for," he growls. I'm speechless on that as he comes to sit next to me. "Anyway, I came to check on you and make sure you're okay."

I go to reply when a small huffing noise grabs my

attention. Gold unzips his coat and pulls out a tiny little creature. It kind of looks like a miniature cow teddy bear, with large floppy ears and massive brown eyes. Its fur is a mixture of brown and white strands that makes him look super soft. The creature huffs again, and Gold places him on the ground, where he runs off into the shadows.

"I couldn't leave him up there, alone," Gold grumbles, watching the creature hide.

We might not be able to see it but we can smell and hear it. It's a noisy but cute little thing.

Luke laughs. "Why exactly are you protecting it, Gov? There are hundreds of them around the prison and thousands in the forest. Most fae eat them."

"Oh my god, they don't really, do they?" I'm absolutely horrified. How could anyone eat something so sweet?

"Oz is fucking different and not like a normal patron creature," Gold states, glowering at Luke and then smiling at me. "You won't believe me, but fuck, Oz has saved my life dozens of times. He can smell poison and warns me not to eat and drink when he knows it will kill me. He has woken me up when inmates have snuck into my room to slit my throat. Oz might be a rodent to the shadowborn world for everyone else, but to me? He's my lifesaver. The least I can do is keep him safe."

This is a surprisingly tender side to Gold I never expected.

"Does he have a friend? Only I'd like an Oz," I ask with a big grin.

"He is one of a kind," Gold drawls, his eyes washing over me.

We all stay in silence for a moment, listening to the raid outside and the screams of the inmates. I hope Axel and Memphis are okay. A thought pops into my head. It's something I've been meaning to ask since I won.

"Gold, can I have a chunk of stone or rock?" I flutter my lashes at him, biting down on my lower lip. Anything to get what I want.

Luke grumbles something, but I can't hear it.

"Why?" Gold asks me, leaning closer. "You want to hit my head with it? Wouldn't be the first time someone's done that."

I clear my throat, wishing he just said yes. "No. A girl I got close to died in the Blood Trials, and her wish was for a headstone for her brother, who also died in the arena. I want to make the headstone the best I can, with their names on it and place it by the tree she told me about."

Palpitations jump in my chest as I wait for his answer.

"I will do it for you," Gold says after a long pause. "Inmates aren't allowed to place headstones or anything on prison grounds, but I am."

"Thank you. I'll write down their names when we get out of here," I say.

"Write them on me," Gold instructs, tugging his sleeve up and finding a magic quill in his coat pocket.

My hands burn as I touch his skin and slowly draw the names there.

Luke clears his throat. "What caused the riot, Gov?"

Gold doesn't even hesitate. "Memphis was found in the lab with his group of twenty guarding him. As you can imagine, a fight broke out. Axel was doing a damn good job distracting me," Gold replies as if this is an everyday occurrence. "I'm sure they're regretting it now."

"Why would they break into the lab?" I question, more confused than enlightened.

Gold remains silent, so Luke answers me. "They probably wanted to find out why the tests are so important and what they do."

"Do you know?" I ask Gold. Surely, he must since it's his prison.

"No."

His curt, one-word answer is clearly all I'm getting for now.

I *will* find out what's going on in that laboratory one way or another. I just need to earn Gold's trust as well as his desire.

I nearly jump out of my skin when Oz climbs up my leg and onto my lap. He curls up into a ball, only his ears sticking out. I gently stroke his back as he drifts off to sleep. In the corner of my eye, I see Gold smile at Oz before snapping his expression back to its usual coldness.

Turns out Governor Gold has a soft side, and its name is Oz.

CHAPTER SEVENTEEN

Izora

To many prisoners, visiting day is the highlight of their week. It should be the one thing I look forward to in this place. When I find out it's my step-sister who's come to pay her respects, my excitement is quick to plummet into dread. I'd prefer to watch paint dry, in all honesty. Hell, I'd rather there was another riot like yesterday than endure a whole hour in my sister's company.

I smooth a hand down my pink blouse, flick a loose thread off my pale grey jeans, and nod to Luke. "Okay. I'm ready to face my executioner again."

Luke chuckles, opening the door that leads to the visiting centre. It's at the front of the prison, located behind security and sandwiched between the Processing Room and what Luke says is the wardens' staffroom. Some inmates are strolling by with black eyes and bruises. Yikes.

The riot must've really kicked off while I was locked up in my room.

"Is Willow really that bad?" he asks as we walk down the corridor.

"Think of the worst person you've ever met," I tell him. "Now imagine three of them squished into a tiny body that's hell-bent on making your life a living misery. That's my sister."

"Got it. Was it her dad that married Grand Warden Greene? Your surnames are different."

It takes a moment to realise he's referring to my mother. "Yeah, he married my mum when I was a kid. I wanted to keep my mum's maiden name. Izora Dawn sounds way more badass than Izora Greene, ya know."

He chuckles, leading me to an open door guarded by various wardens. I can already hear the chattering from outside. I step into the visiting centre. The room is extremely bland and bare minimum. On one side, there's a couple of water coolers, and the other has plastic chairs huddled around coffee tables. Most of the seats have already been occupied while a group of wardens patrols the floor.

"She's over there," Luke says, pointing to the chair by the window. "You get up to an hour. I'll stand by your table."

"I can't wait for this. Really. I'm overjoyed," I drawl, rolling my eyes.

I barely reach Willow when she pounces off her chair and gasps, "Oh, Izy!"

She throws out her arms and envelopes me into a false embrace. I look around, wondering who she's putting this show on for. My step-sister has hugged me probably twice in all the years I've known her. Even then, it was just to whisper insults in my ear so that I'd lash out and get grounded.

After putting on such a realistic performance of sisterly love, Willow sits back in her chair, ushering me over to the one across from her. She casts Luke a glance beside our table, his hands behind his back, eyes scanning the room along with the other wardens.

"Is that Derek Luke?" she whispers to me, pointing her head at him. I nod and she giggles. "Oh my gosh. Just wait until the girls hear about this."

"When you're quite done checking my warden out, Willow, tell me why you're here."

She straightens her back, sitting the prim and proper way my mother always wanted me to. "Why, I came to see you, of course. You're my sis, and I've been worried about you."

"So worried you never wrote a letter?"

Her throat works, and she snaps her jaw shut. Choosing to ignore my comment, she flicks her long, white hair over one shoulder and says, "How are things in here? Has anyone, you know, made you drop the soap in the shower yet?"

It's Luke who laughs at the ridiculous comment. He quickly clears his throat and pulls himself together. I grin at him, then face my stupid sister.

"No, Willow. I haven't been peter gazing in prison."

"Thank Selena. I'll let Mother know once we find her."

My pulse spikes. "Find her?"

"That's why I came here." She looks over shoulder and around the room, then lowers her voice. "Mother has been missing since you were sentenced. Father and I thought she needed space and perhaps went to visit our home in Helios, but...she hasn't come back and the staff there haven't seen her since we were last there. Do you have any idea where she could've gone? Father is worried sick."

I feel like the wind has been kicked from my sails. It takes every scrap of willpower not to lose my shit in front of so many people. My mother has been missing for weeks, and I'm just being told about it? My mind races with a million different scenarios. The most painful one of all is... what if the wardens who took me away have now taken her?

"When and where was she last seen?" I ask in a low voice, an attempt to mask the rage that is only seconds from erupting.

"The day you were sentenced. Once they took you away, Mother stayed behind to beseech the Grand Warden. She never came home that night."

So the last person to see her might have been the warden that sentenced me? I think I know who can help me.

I stand from my chair, but Willow grabs my wrist. "Wait! You can't just leave. You never answered my question. Where do you think she's gone?"

"Oh, please," I snarl, scrunching my face in disgust.

184

"You and your dad have been waiting for my mum to just 'disappear' for years now so you can have her fortune. Don't you dare sit here pretending to be concerned about her!"

Luke takes my arm and steers me away before I make an even bigger scene. I'm shaking from head-to-foot and I feel sick, disgusted by the news. My mother might have been cold and distant with me growing up, and we are a far cry from a normal mother-daughter relationship, but she's still my mother and only living relative. She would never just up and disappear. Her job is far too important to her.

"She's been taken," I tell Luke, my voice trembling. "I know it."

He pulls us into a corner of the hallway that's quiet. "I'll see what I can find out."

"Thank you..." The tremble in my voice catches my bottom lip, and I bite down hard on it. "I need to let off some steam."

I think he knows where this is going because he looks away and shakes his head, clearly troubled.

"Don't do it," he begs in a whisper, closing his eyes. "Your life is worth more, jaybird."

That may be true, but right now, I need another reward.

And the only way to get that is to sign up for this week's Blood Trials.

CHAPTER EIGHTEEN

Izora

AFTER PUTTING MY NAME DOWN FOR SATURDAY, I practically charge into Scott's classroom without even checking to see if he's teaching anyone. Thankfully, he's alone, his nose buried in a worn-out copy of the *Book of Zorya*.

He pushes off the edge of his desk and smiles at me, closing the book. "Morning, Izora. How are you today?"

I march right up to him, requesting, "I need your help."

Scott sets the book down and rests his hands on my shoulders, searching my expression. My professor looks extremely sexy today in his black tie and slacks. His cream shirt is rolled up at the sleeves, showing off his many tattoos. Unfortunately, I don't take the time I usually do to check him out whenever I see him. My mind is fixed on someone else.

"Anything," he whispers.

"My mum has gone missing. She's apparently been gone for weeks, but Willow only told me just now. I'm really worried. Could you ask around about her?"

I know I shouldn't be asking him for favours, but I need this.

Scott sucks a breath in through his teeth. "I heard a high up went missing. I didn't know it was your mum," he replies with a frown before pulling me into a hug. "But of course I will do anything I can."

"Thank you," I mumble against his chest, enjoying his arms around me.

I'm so thankful he no longer holds back. I used to daydream about him holding me like this, which seems like a lifetime ago.

"Gage Micheals is waiting for you in the next room," he tells me, and I eye him curiously. "I think once a month you should see him and talk out anything you need. Gage is good at his job, damn good, and you've been through hell. I think it'll do you good."

"I don't know," I reply. There was a reason I avoided therapy at the academy, and I don't want to start now. Then Abbie's face and final moments flash before my eyes, and I pause.

"Please?" he murmurs and it's surprisingly really cute.

Cute enough that I find myself nodding in agreement.

He grins and walks me to the door. Before he knocks to ask Luke to open the door, he kisses my cheek and his lips linger for a moment more than necessary, his beard tickling my cheek. I close my eyes and enjoy the brief token of affection before he knocks. In a matter of seconds, Luke has the door open, his eyes swiftly checking me over for any injury before looking at Scott.

"Izora is spending the day with Gage. Could you take her next door?" Scott asks coolly.

Luke eyes him with disdain laced in jealousy as he reaches for my hand, all but dragging me from the room and slamming the door shut in Scott's face.

"You don't have to stay out here all day. I will be safe with Gage," I say, certain Luke has some things he wants to do. Other than at night once I've fallen asleep, he's always at my side. Every single day. "Don't you have days off?"

"You're never safe here. Never," Luke grumbles. "And if you knew what I've had to protect you from so far, you'd never sleep."

"Had to protect me?" I spit out, pulling my hand from his. "I'm sorry your job is so inconvenient."

He knocks on Gage's door twice before looking at me as I shake with anger. "This was never just a job from day one. You couldn't be just a job even if I wished to Selena to make it so."

"Ah, Izora, please come in," Gage answers the door before I can throw a reply at Luke.

The warden eyes me like I'm the spawn of Satan as I turn to Gage, plastering a fake smile on my lips and heading inside. His room is pretty plain with two worn grey sofas. A fake green-leafed plant stands in the corner of the room by the window, even when it doesn't need light. Two glass side tables rest next to the facing sofas, and each one has an empty glass on them with a bottle of water.

"I'm Gage Micheals. We didn't see each other much at Shadowborn Academy, did we?" Gage says as he waves at one of the sofas for me to sit down while he takes the other. I cross my legs under me as I wait for his next response to fill the silence. "Vina must have been wrong. When we talk about you, she always says you're brave and chatty. She wants to be like you, I suspect."

"I like Vina as she is," I mutter.

Gage is good. He's already using my weak spots to make me lower my defence. Dammit.

"So do I, and she deeply misses you," he replies, and we both smile. "Professor Mune informed me that you entered the Blood Trials here at the prison and won. That must have been difficult for you."

"Extremely," I reply and the next words spill out my mouth before I can catch them. "Not because of the actual event but the deaths I caused and the one death I couldn't stop."

His head tilts to the side as he crosses his arms, leaning back. "Tell me about the death you couldn't stop."

"Her name was Abbie, and I trained her as part of my job here at the prison. I knew from the second I met her that she would die in the Blood Trials." I look away, focusing on the plant. It reminds me of being back in the rainforest and all the screams. "Vina lied when she said I was brave. I wasn't brave enough to tell Abbie she was weak and that she should pull out. I didn't want to break her dreams," I whisper, feeling tears in the corner of my eyes. "The truth is, Abbie reminded me of myself, like a much younger version of me. Except I could learn how to fight and protect myself with years of training, and she didn't have that. She had one week."

Gage crosses his legs, his light brown eyes fixed on me. "We all have to accept that we have no control over other people's lives or actions. Abbie made the choice to sign up. Abbie decided what she wanted and most likely understood that death would be her ending as it will be for all of us. Some sooner than others. You cannot blame yourself for choices that were out of your control."

"But what if I could've made them pick the better choice?"

He shakes his head slowly. "We still can't control the outcome. Who's to say that one wouldn't have turned out worse in the end? Whatever happens to someone happens for a reason. It's their path and journey, not ours."

"I guess you're right," I say, nodding my head but it's still not easy to accept. A tissue appears in front of me, and I look up to see Gage offering me it. I smile thankfully as I take it and clean my eyes. "I would like to come back but today I have to go back to my room and work on the headstone I've been making for Abbie and her brother. Once I'm done, I can move on from this."

"Next time we should discuss the darkness in your eyes, Izora. Even though the collar stops your magic, it does not mean it isn't building inside you. Dark emotions make Shadowborns more powerful, and when you are free, you don't want to lose control. We have to find a way for you to come back."

Now it's my turn to shake my head. "I'm not a shadowborn anymore, and I never lied in court. I am a light fae, and my powers are more in control than they have ever felt. That has nothing to do with this collar and everything to with the fact I know in my soul I'm not evil. I did nothing wrong."

I give a faint smile before I leave the room, and Luke wordlessly follows behind me.

I don't need therapy… I just need to find the person I'm meant to be.

CHAPTER NINETEEN

Izora

"**D**ON'T DO IT."

I briefly close my eyes, hating the pain I hear in Axel's voice. "I need to. I have no choice anyway. You know yourself that once you sign up to the Blood Trials, there's no backing out."

He scrunches his face at me, the veins in his neck pulsing with unease. "This ain't like the usual ones. It's a duo which means two trials on one day. That's twice the players and twice the usual amount of blood. You don't wanna be part of that, Izora."

I swallow my own unease and put on a brave face for him. Inmates are gathering outside the doors to the Blood Trials, and there's at least forty of them. I've never seen so many players. I'd be lying if I said I wasn't afraid. But there's no other solution. I need these rewards. I need to do this. Closing the distance between us, I cup the side of his face, but Axel grabs my wrist.

"Why do you need to, cutie?"

His voice is so unusually small that it kills me a little inside. Yet part of me still hesitates to tell the truth. I trust Axel more than any other inmate in this prison. Memphis has become a friend of mine, too, but Axel is the one who's beginning to have my heart as well as my trust.

"It's my mum," I say, and Axel slowly lowers my hand but keeps hold of my wrist. "She's been missing for a while now and I need help to find her. I need Gold's help."

"*Gold…*" He practically sneers the name. "We've told you not to trust him."

"Who says I trust him? I'm merely abusing his power."

That gets a little laugh from Axel. He slides his thumb over the back of my hand before letting me go, just as Luke appears at my side with a note.

"From Mune," he grumbles, handing me a little scroll.

I unroll the parchment and read the note. My eyes widen with every word. My mother is safe! Scott has been able to contact her, and he'll tell me all about it when I see him tomorrow. I can't believe it. The relief is shattering and I clench the scroll in my hand, thankful she's alive and safe. However, this now means I no longer need a reward. Well, that's not entirely true. I can always do with rewards, and I can use this one to get closer to Gold. Despite being his neighbour, I rarely see him and that needs to change.

Besides, I can't pull out of the Blood Trials without forfeiting my life.

And that will never happen.

I tuck the scroll into the back pocket of my jeans and

look up at the guys. They're both glaring venomously at each other, and I just catch the last of Axel's sentence.

"...her blood on your hands."

The doors open and the players hurry inside. I should probably go too if I want to get the best weapons.

"I'm going to be okay," I tell the guys firmly. "Just have some faith in me and enjoy the show."

Before they can argue, I pivot on my heel and make my way into the hall. I don't want them to see that I'm also beginning to secretly doubt myself.

Can't be weak, got to be strong.

I repeat the mantra while Warden Kyle gives his speech to the new players. As soon as he stops droning on, I slip into my locker room and assess the clothing to garner what the landscape will be. Going by the familiar catsuit and trainers, it's the rainforest again. I'm actually a little relieved. It was easier to navigate than the arctic.

I'm dressed and equipped with my weapons in no time. I decided to go for a bow this time, since I've always been good at archery, along with my usual daggers and sword. Before I slide through the hole that drops me into the arena, I grab what looks like a bunch of small grenades and clip the belt above my daggers. No idea what they do, but hopefully they explode things.

The familiar mechanical voice returns, telling everyone what to do.

Grab your orb, slide down the hole after the countdown. May Selena be with you.

I just want to get in already.

"Three...two...one."

I'm first to jump through and reach the other side, but I don't land where I thought I would. Instead of a net catching my fall, my body plunges into a swamp that tries to suck me in. I thrust my arms out and kick my legs, clawing my way out from the wet dirt. The mud covers most of my body and hair. At least I won't need to rub myself in it this time.

The sound of others landing in the swamp are quick to jolt me into motion. I haul my legs through the thick water and dart into the trees, just as a knife slices into the branch hanging by my head.

These trees are noticeably different from the ones in the other rainforest. They're much taller and their canopies are thicker, barely letting in any slivers of sunlight. The trunks are wrapped in vines that crawl all the way down to the roots and spread out into the rotting vegetation below. This landscape is more jungle-like than anything.

I head further into the trees, prepared to fight for my life at any second. Monkeys swoosh through the trees around me, their movements sending an array of leaves fluttering to the ground while they hoot at each other. The exotic sounds of the jungle are almost relaxing. The fact that I'm currently being hunted like wild boar certainly puts a damper on the mood, but if I was back home listening to this, I'd be asleep in no time.

The scent of magic surges in the dense air, crackling through the leaves. I use it as a guide to track the way to where I *think* my next clue is. My suit is keeping my body cool for the most part, but the jungle itself is stiflingly warm and suffocating. Everywhere I go, leaves slap against my body in an effort to trap me.

When I can no longer detect the magic, I consider shifting into my wolf since her senses are stronger. But a scream not far causes me to pauses in my tracks.

"Give us the orb," Tyler bellows, and the scream becomes a cry.

"You don't need it. You don't need it!"

"Just kill the kid and take it."

The order comes from Coen, right before the boy's cry turns into an ear-splitting shriek and then… silence.

A tendril of fear creeps into me. I don't want to face the pack until I know what this challenge entails. I shift into a white raven and perch on a nearby branch, watching as Coen, Tyler, and the three other guys trudge through the vegetation. It's the first time I don't see them all decked out in orbs. Holding the one he just stole, Tyler pauses in a ray of sunlight to get a better look at the orb. It shrinks in the palm of his hand and transforms into a small crystal vial. It reminds me of the ones students wear at the academy, the ones that glow and binds to their magic.

"What the fuck am I to do with this?"

One of the guys peers over his shoulder. "Who knows. The orbs only turn into something you might need. Could need it now, at the end, or never. Just keep a hold of it."

Now that's interesting. The orbs aren't to gain points here but to give us something we need. That also means we don't necessarily need to kill other players to win. But I guess Coen and his pack will still want to claim every orb for their trophy collection.

One day, I'm going to kill them all for good. I'm almost tempted to shift back and shoot an arrow through Coen's skull. But I need to bide my time. I wait until they leave before flying down. With the scent of magic scarcely detectable, I consider remaining in my bird-form and following the pack, but there are far too many predators here and unless I'm in the sky, I'm easy prey.

Certain that I'm alone, I return to my human form and continue my trek on foot. I'm careful to keep a safe distance from the pack. I figure they're headed where everyone else is—to get the grand prize—and they're more experienced at this than I am. I wouldn't be surprised if they already know where to go.

I slap a mosquito from my neck. *These damn things are everywhere!* I'm careful about where I tread, making sure I step only in the guys' footprints. Unfortunately, this means I need to take time to watch where I'm going, which slows up my process, and their scents and voices are beginning to fade.

The sweat gathering on my brow slides down my face. I wipe the droplets with the only part of my sleeve that isn't covered in mud. As I move my arm away, a whoosh of cool air shoots past my ear. My feet root to the spot. A shimmering orange dart punctures a tree not six feet away. That's not a good sign.

I duck down into the foliage and shrug the bow off

my shoulder, swiftly knocking an arrow and taking aim. In the shadows of the trees across the clearing, an almost naked man emerges. His face is painted in white stripes and he has feathers and bones woven in his long, straggly hair. He's definitely not a prison inmate. Maybe he's part of the simulation? Either way, if it comes down to one of us dying, it's going to be him.

Releasing the arrow, I watch it sail through the air towards his face.

The man catches it like it's nothing.

He opens his mouth to reveal severely rotted, gapped teeth, and lets out a strange, slightly strangled sound that I think is supposed to be a laugh. Then he just snaps my arrow in half, dumps it to the ground, and lifts a small flute to his mouth.

Okay. Looks like I'll have to fight face to face.

Or maybe I could just like my wolf eat him.

The latter is more tempting. I carefully stand from my crouched position to shift into my wolf. The branches falling and cracking behind the man diverts his attention. It's just what I need. I smile, preparing to let my wolf take over. But then Axel appears out of nowhere and thrusts a sword through the man's neck quicker than he can blow his little flute. He drops to his knees and vanishes into dust.

"You looked you needed help," Axel says, a slow smile creeping onto his lips. "So here I am."

CHAPTER TWENTY

Izora

I PRACTICALLY RUN OVER AND THROW MYSELF AXEL'S arms, demanding, "How in the name of Selena did you get in here?"

Axel hugs me, his big hand sliding down to the small of my back. Only then do I notice his tight black shirt and similar material trousers. Big ass swords hang on his back and the straps crisscross over his chest. "I wanted to make sure my cutie gets outta here alive. I pulled some strings. Bada bing, bada boom."

I gawk at him. He's literally risking his life…for me? Tears gather in my eyes. I don't think anyone's ever done something like this for me.

"I can't believe it," I whisper, pressing my face into his shirt.

Axel presses a kiss on the top of my head. "I know. It's kinda romantic, the two of us here, in the middle of the jungle…" His hand slides further down and lands on my ass.

I push away from him, grinning. "For real, though, we're being hunted like we're tonight's supper. If you're here to help, we need to find the prize." Gesturing to where I last saw the pack go, I say, "I was hunting Coen. Wherever they went, I'm sure the prize is there."

He nods. "Then let's go. But watch out for that."

I follow his gaze to the monstrous snake slithering around a swooping branch overhead. Axel chuckles and steps around me, leading the way through the trees.

I carefully follow in his wake, mindful of the reptile as it makes its way to the other side. "You know, I'm glad I'm not scared of snakes or anything like that. This would be real inconvenient otherwise."

"And are you scared of them, cutie?"

"Only the poisonous ones. And spiders. They creep me the fuck out. I think it's the legs, the way they scuttle."

He laughs, cutting through a barrier of leaves. "In that case, you better focus ahead instead of down."

"That's what I've been doing but now…you've made me…wanna…check…Oh, my sweet Zorya fuck!"

The entire ground is covered in insects and critters scuttling about. I'd bet my reward there's a big motherfucker spider hiding somewhere, just waiting to pounce onto my face.

Selena, if you're listening, please don't throw any tarantulas my way. I need to win this game, not die from a heart attack.

My mood, however, has been considerably lightened since Axel's arrival. It feels good to walk with him in an area that that isn't *quite* the prison. This might be fake and all, with an air of impending doom looming over us, but it's nice to spend time alone.

Plus, he's a much better tracker than I am, pointing out things I never would have noticed. I wonder if he's part fae. He doesn't have the typical features of one, but then neither does Gold and I know he's Draconian, who are descended from fae.

I fall into step with Axel, telling him, "Apparently the orbs aren't to win points here but to give us something we need."

He scoffs, cutting the leaves away with added force. "That's normally how the duos go. It's to encourage the players to fight each other from the get-go instead of running away or some shit. The more orbs, the more mini prizes you'll get, which'll get you to the end faster. Nasty as fuck incentive, if you ask me."

"Yeah," I agree, glancing at the ground. So far no monster creepy crawlies. "Have you ever competed in a duo?"

Axel freezes at the question, his arm still raised to chop down more foliage. "Once. I lost my best friend that day, Eli. He was Memphis' partner. Nearly destroyed him."

Sadness clogs in my throat at the words. I can't imagine how horrific that must have been for them both. Losing Abbie was hard enough for me. But to lose your best friend? Your soulmate?

"How long ago was that?" I ask in a whisper.

He resumes walking again, his shoulders bulking. "Four years ago."

"You've been here that long? Why?"

I know this is a touchy subject for Axel, and I don't really expect him to answer. I just hate the thought of him wasting away in here. He doesn't deserve that. The more I think about it, the more I applaud him and Memphis starting a riot.

Axel bends over and picks a stone off the ground. I watch him throw it into the tree, hitting a bird that was perched on a branch. I gasp in shock, horrified, until the bird's head rolls off and mechanical sparks shoot from the neck. So that's how they record everything—through decoy animals?

"Look, there's fresh tracks," I say, receiving Axel's hint loud and clear. It isn't safe to talk about certain things here. "It looks like the pack shifted into a run. Maybe they found another kid to murder."

"Or maybe they were chased by the natives that live here," he counters, kneeling down to inspect them. "Ah, see. Bare footprints."

"You're a smart cookie, Axel. I'm glad you came to help me."

We follow the tracks down a moss-covered sloop to a creek. There's a spot of land on the other side and jagged rocks stained in blood, but it's the middle that grabs our attention. Coen and five other wolves are ripping through natives like they are cattle. The natives are all circled around a glowing object. There must be at least one hundred of them protecting it, but the pack are quickly chewing their way through them.

"We should sneak behind them and let Coen be the distraction," Axel murmurs. "Get your wolf to follow me."

Only then does Axel shift into a black panther with thick, long teeth and gleaming blue eyes. I shift into my wolf after a flicker of hesitation and follow Axel through the trees to the back of the creek. His panther jumps down the rocks and my wolf mimics his moves until we reach the bottom. We both shift back and readjust our weapons when several of the natives notice us.

"Time to show off my skills," Axel cockily states, pulling out his swords.

I roll my eyes and grab my bow, shooting the native closest to me. I aim for an area I doubt he'd expect, right on the ass, and he explodes into dust.

Grabbing three more arrows, I thank Selena for the archery skills that my mother taught me. "You attack and I will cover you."

"Got it," Axel shouts and rushes over to the natives. He moves with perfectly concise movements, tearing through them with an almost fiendish fury, dropping their gutted remains to the ground before they turn to dust.

I shoot the three arrows before Axel even gets close, taking down two of the natives and just missing a wolf. We work effortlessly as a team. Axel kills one after the other, and damn he's skilled, every blow expertly delivered, never missing a beat. I throw one of my grenades, curious to see what it does. A cloud of pink smoke wraps around two natives and one of the wolves, then they are on the ground, screaming and rotting into ash. I throw more of them and shoot at least ten arrows around Axel before I realise it's too quiet. The natives all are dead or running away, but where is…

Coen's wolf lunges on top of Axel, knocking him to the ground, and then he tears into Axel's shoulder.

"*No!*" I scream, my entire body filling with insurmountable fear. I pull another arrow and shoot. It hits his upper side instead of his throat, and Coen keeps ripping into Axel's shoulder like it's a big slab of meat.

"Get the orb!" Axel roars, but I rush over to him, dropping my bow. I pull my daggers out and I don't even blink as I jump onto Coen's wolf, sliding my daggers into his neck again and again. He tries to fight me off for a moment before his body collapses on Axel.

"Axel, no, no, no," I mutter repeatedly as I haul Coen's dead wolf off him and see all the blood over his top. To my relief, Axel is alive, flinching with every tiny movement as I help him into a sitting position.

"I told you to get the orb, Izora."

"Yeah, well, I never listen. We get the orb together and get out of here," I snap, pulling him to his feet. He groans just as I see his orb on his leg roll off his leg and onto the floor, changing into a vial.

"The game gives us what we need," Axel says, seeing the same thing as me.

I pick it up, flick off the lid and help him drink it. Before my very eyes, the bloodstains disappear and the ripped flesh on his shoulder is gone. I grin at him, and he smiles back, shoving me playfully on the arm. We both run to the prize with our hands linked. Axel places them on the orb at the same time as he looks down and kisses me. The orb, the trials and everything blurs as Axel's soft lips claim mine passionately, and holy Selena, he's an even better kisser than he is a fighter. I completely forget about where I am, lost in his arms and captive to his kiss.

"Congratulations," Gold's pissed off voice drawls as Axel breaks the kiss and winks at me. I don't even look up at Gold for a moment as I try to catch my breath, and think of something I need as a prize. "What do you want?"

"You know what I want," Axel states and walks off, throwing me a naughty grin over his shoulder. He joins Memphis and all the other inmates applauding and cheering away.

I finally lift my head to meet Gold's eyes. Nothing but burning fury lingers in those molten depths. I know what I need to ask for now.

"I want a date with you. In your room, just the two of us," I state firmly, holding his gaze with unwavering determination.

This is how I get closer to gain my freedom back and end the Blood Trials in the process.

His eyes widen. For a moment, he considers my words with an amused smirk, then he just laughs.

"Done," he says, flashing a smile before he pivots on his heel and leaves the room.

I watch him go, smiling for a different reason entirely.

Gold has no idea what he's agreed to. He might as well have just let the devil in his home.

CHAPTER TWENTY-ONE

Izora

"FOR YOU," A GUARD WHO ISN'T LUKE grumbles, shoving a gold box into my hands.

The box is large enough that I have to use both my hands to hold it steady. This guard is bold, with a large stomach bulging over his trousers and a scrunched-up pig-like face. His nose is crooked like it's been broken a few times before.

"Where is Luke?"

The guard just frowns at me. "Warden Luke is off for the next few hours. Governer Gold expects you in his room in half an hour," the guard replies and slams the door shut on me.

I guess Luke needs some time off...but why does that make me worry? I've not seen him have a day off in, well, forever. I place the box on the kitchen side and tug the sparkling gold ribbon bow off before opening the lid. Inside, a black note with my name in gold ink lies on top of silky gold fabric. Is there anything that isn't gold in here? I pick the note up and sweep my eyes over the elegant handwriting:

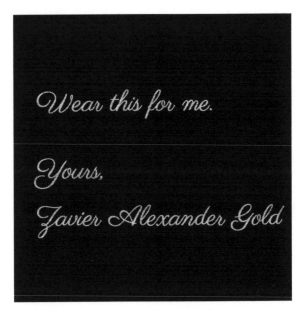

Wear this for me.

Yours,

Xavier Alexander Gold

I put the sweet but commanding note down and pick up the dress. It falls to the floor by my feet. The silk material will be tight but it feels like pure and utter luxury. I don't even think as I strip out of my clothes and slide the dress onto my freshly showered body. I look at my reflection in the mirror on the vanity. Shame about my collar, but other than that, I look and feel beautiful. The gown has a sweetheart neckline and the back is a crisscross of silk ties that run all the way down to just above my coccyx. I undo my braids, letting the curls cascade over my back. The gold goes perfectly with my skin tone and silver hair, and I hope he likes how I look.

I *need* him to like it.

And the more I think about it, the more I realise I need him to like me, not just to end the Blood Trials, but for another reason I yet don't want to understand or admit.

I find a pair of silver heels in my wardrobe and slip them on. By the time I've had a glass of water, the half-hour is already up. The guard opens my door before I get to it, and he's silent as I walk past him. There are seven steps between my room and Gold's. So close and yet he's always been so far.

My heels click-clack against the floor as I make my way over. The heart palpitations jumping into my throat take me by surprise. Why am I nervous? I was the one who wanted this. I tap my knuckles on the wood and wait for what feels like forever until Gold opens the door. He just pauses, as if the whole world has stopped.

It feels exactly the same way to me.

Gold has always been a beautiful man and turns the heads of many in this prison. But this is the first time I've seen him not wearing a suit which somehow makes him look sexier. I cast my eyes over his lean body, biting my lower lip. The sleeves of his black shirt are rolled-up to the elbow and the hem is tucked into his black slacks. A gold tie and braces that stretch over his torso complete the look, along with a pair of black wingtip shoes and a silver watch gleaming on his wrist. His hair is styled away from his freshly shaved face, and the tattoos seem to make his eyes all that more expressive.

Gold's throat works as he, too, looks at me. "You look otherworldly, Izora Dawn."

His compliment makes me shiver just from the raw, deep masculine tone.

The desire in every word and how my knees threaten to go weak from one sentence.

Gods, it's hard to keep my head on around him.

"Thank you," I eventually reply and nod my head towards his room. "Do you not let all your dates in?"

"Only the beautiful ones I want to stare at longer," he smoothly answers, stepping aside.

Flashing him a grin, I enter his room, his personal space, and his hand flattens against my back. The strips of silk do nothing to block the heat from his hand, or how good it feels. I inwardly shake my head. *Focus. This is just part of my plan.* I sweep my gaze around his room, taking everything in. The layout is the same as my suite, but this home is all Gold's. Weapons adorn the wall around the blazing fireplace. A dining table set for two rests on the middle of the floor with candles, wine glasses and bottles laid out on the surface. His sleeping area is on the platform to the left of the room, just like mine, but his bed is a dark wooden four-poster with silk sheets. The leather straps tied to each of the posts don't escape my notice, and my insides quiver.

Gold presses his hand lightly and leads me over to the table before pulling out a chair for me. I sit down and he moves to the seat at the other end, waving a hand, and I taste the magic in the air just before two silver plates filled with bread and cheese appear, melted to perfection. It's just enough since I've already eaten today. A small pot of onion chutney rests next to the cheese and suddenly the glasses on the table fill themselves up with red wine.

"I love light magic and how endless it is," I say as I pick up the wine glass. "Are you a full fae or half?"

"Half, and no, I don't have wings. I seem to have inherited my father's power but none of his looks other than the eyes," he replies with a wolfish grin. "Not all fae have this gift. Only the Draconians."

He's being surprisingly more open and direct than I thought he'd be. This plan might work after all.

I take a sip of my wine, my eyes intent on his. "I heard the Draconians never mate outside their race and nothing about their power is an illusion, not like with the fae," I tell him, conveying the rumours and whispers from Shadowborn Academy and my mother. She did always love the dragons and said they were a beautiful but deadly race in our world.

We can look at them, admire them, but never touch.

Ever.

And now I'm sitting across from one.

"My people like to pretend they didn't come from fae. It's a shitty pretence though," he counters with a dark chuckle. "They love to fuck the fae as much as any race."

"Tell me how you became the governor," I ask, tilting my head to the side.

"Simple. I got into a fight one night and killed three Keepers."

He doesn't even falter when he says that. It sends a shiver through my body. I guess I can't be appalled anymore. I've killed people, too.

"While serving as a general in the Draconian army, I took my men out for a drink at the Zorya Inn in Helios," he explains, swirling the wine in his glass. "Things got ugly real quick when a bunch of Keepers decided to give us some trouble. One thing led to another. I landed myself in a holding facility for a while. The previous governor of this place died during that time and Ulric came to visit me."

"The Light Fae King?" I ask as my eyes widen, believing every word.

"The very one." He chuckles, rubbing his chin. "But he wasn't my king then and still isn't. I punched him in the face when he said I was a mess."

I gasp, wondering how exactly he's still alive. The fae royals are known to be vicious and never allowed any form of disrespect towards them to go unpunished.

"Anyway, I was the unlucky fuck he was looking for and so he hired me. The rest is history."

I chuckle with him, even though my cheeks burn at hearing him say fuck. I love how he says that. We eat in silence for a while, a surprisingly comfortable one, until we are both finished. The plate disappears and in its place, a bowl of vanilla ice cream appears.

"How did you know that's my favourite?"

"Luke happened to mention it once," he replies with a cheeky grin as I dig into the ice cream, but he doesn't have any. "And you can thank me later for making your personal guard take a day off today."

"You didn't have to do that," I comment, though I'm relieved it wasn't Luke's choice to leave.

"I want you alone and Luke is not going to let that happen. Sometimes I feel he puts his obsession with you over his commands from me," he all but growls, and his eyes flash green for a moment.

"He isn't here, he is?" I swallow the ice cream down and look around the room.

Gold chuckles and leans forward, resting his head on his joint hands. "Tell me why you wanted a date first, little Izora. I highly doubt you simply want to fuck me tonight." He slowly drifts his eyes over my body and my breath hitches. "But we can still do that later. I've been looking for someone to occupy my time with."

"I-I…" Clearing my throat a few times, I get myself under control. "I want you to end the Blood Trials and make it safe again. Shadowborns are not worthless and most here are not guilty enough to die in such a barbaric way."

A dark look drifts over his face. "What makes you think I have any true control over a prison I myself am locked in?"

"You're trapped here as well?" I whisper, my eyes bulging in their sockets.

He doesn't answer me per se. "The only way out of

217

here is to let the lab do a test on you. The test I stopped them from doing because I very much doubt whatever they are looking for is going to be any good for the winner."

A sour taste fills my mouth and lingers in the back of my throat. Now I know for sure there is something bigger at play here in this prison and it doesn't just involve Gold. It makes what happened to me all the more real. Maybe I'm not the only one who was falsely accused and forced to come here.

"If you're not the one controlling the prison, then there's someone out there who is. What do they want with us? What are they testing for?"

Gold's eyes narrow into slits, a tell-tale sign that he's getting annoyed. "Don't search the darkness of this prison too much, Izora. Some monsters and secrets need to be kept in the dark."

"Like you and me?" I whisper, holding his gaze.

Gold gets up and I stand to meet him as he walks around the table.

He leans in, never quite touching me. "You won't ever be my secret, Izora. When I take you as mine"—he moves closer so that our lips are only inches away—"the whole world will know who you belong to."

I search his eyes that seem to darken in the moments before I close the gap and kiss him. His lips press against mine. The first brush is like a drug, addictive and seductive in the worst possible way. And then he deepens the kiss and picks me up with his giant hands like I weigh nothing. I groan as he drops my ass on the edge of the table, and I naturally part my legs for him, wanting him closer as his kisses continue to make me wet. His hands slide between us and he pushes up my dress, rubbing his thumb all the way up my leg and to the crux of my thigh.

Gods, I want him.

He doesn't stop until his whole hand is cupping me and he can no doubt feel how wet I am for him.

"No panties. Good girl," he growls against my lips, his fingers sliding down to my clit. He rubs me with the pad of his thumb, the motions slow and torturous, and I moan, my body filling with desire. His other hand pushes me back onto the table so I'm lying down, and then his face is between my legs. His tongue replaces his thumb, torturing my clit with swift, dexterous flicks. He slides two fingers into my pussy, and I gasp, clenching around him. "Fuck you taste like the best fucking thing in the world. So tight, so perfect. So, so fucking mine."

I'm losing the will to not come just from his dirty talk alone. I arch my back against the table, practically face-fucking him as I push myself into his mouth. His wicked tongue sucks on my clit, his fingers thrust in and out quickly, and the pressure building inside of me explodes. I cum hard and fast around him, my hands digging into his hair as I let out my moans. In a daze, he picks me off the table and sets me down on the floor, pulling my dress down and slapping my ass with a sexy smirk gracing his wet lips. I can barely stand from the aftershocks of what was just the best orgasm of my life.

"Thanks for dessert and a sexy as fuck date," he tells

me, guiding me to the door and waving his hand over the lock.

"Umm…" I glance at his crotch, glad to see he's got an erection, but confused by my dismissal. Wait, is this date over? Surely he wants me to help him get off. "Don't you want me to…?"

He chuckles, opening the door for me. The cold air from the corridor is a welcome relief against my flushed skin. He leans down and kisses me hard on the lips, forcing me to take a step back.

"Next time, I'm making you mine, Izora."

He winks and then signals the warden who escorted me here. I bet the guy heard everything, but I don't care. I look intently into Gold's eyes before smirking and turning away.

Next time, I'm making Gold realise something very important.

Only I decide who I belong to.

CHAPTER TWENTY-TWO

Izora

THE PRISON IS TENSE AS LUKE AND I WALK DOWN the stairs. For some reason, I feel more than the usual amount of stares with every step, and I don't think it's because I won the Blood Trials again. I look up to the top floor and the wardens all appear busy as normal. Gold is on his throne, staring ahead at something. Nothing seems too out of sorts.

When we reach the bottom, Coen, Tyler, and the rest the Pack of Assholes are waiting with their arms crossed, cruel smirks all around.

"Move out the way. Now!" Luke growls, his angry and dark tone giving me all kinds of goosebumps. Coen keeps his eyes on mine, a silent warning he is always here and cannot be killed, then he nods his head to the side and leaves with his fun little gang.

"Don't you just wish whatever they did to get in here

was given a death sentence instead?" I whisper to Luke as he tugs me to the side and we head towards my lesson with Scott.

"Coen murdered four women, all eighteen and all shadowborns," he quietly tells me. "He got sentenced here and on his way, he also killed two Shadow Wardens by cuttin' their throats out... with his teeth. He's brutal and playin' a game which involves you, but don't worry."

"Don't worry about the throat biter?" I gulp. "You saw him in the arena. That guy has serious issues with me."

"You're never goin' back in that arena. And if he comes near you again, I'll kill him," Luke warns darkly, keeping his eyes on mine.

The prison, the walls, and even the floor disappear from my senses as Luke gets all my attention in less than a second. I really stare at him for a moment, hearing my heart pitter-pattering away inside my chest, almost like it wants to escape and fall into Luke's arms.

Gross metaphor but true nonetheless.

Luke is gorgeous. I've always noticed that and anyone who says otherwise is in denial. He has this playboy, rugged quality to him that I love, and yet he's also super possessive.

And darker than his looks suggest he might be.

"I know of Shadow Wardens and how all wardens are given wives or husbands when they turn a certain age. Have you been told who you will marry?" I ask, saying the words I need to without really saying them at all.

Wardens and Shadowborns don't belong together.

It's forbidden for his kind... and even sex is frowned upon.

His jaw tightens as we come around a corridor and he stops us right outside Scott's door. He leans over me, his hand flattening on the wooden door by my head.

"Shadow Wardens don't belong here and yet here I am. I've broken fuck knows how many rules to keep you safe so far..." He pauses, leaning in closer just for a second. "I will break all the rules this world has if I decide you're mine. Just be ready to fight the world at my side when I do."

"Luke, you're out of your mind," I say in exaggerated surprise, but dammit, I like this possessive side of his.

"And yet you aren't runnin' away. What does that say?" he asks with a dark chuckle, straightening up before the cameras turn our way. Sneaky warden. Luke knocks on the door twice before taking another step back, but I'm still in a daze as Scott opens the door and lets me inside.

"How was your week?" Scott asks me as he shuts the door on Luke, with unnecessary harshness, might I add.

Poor Luke.

I sit down at the desk right at the front. I've been eager to speak with Scott since I received his letter, but he told me to wait until today. Now I can finally find out what happened to her.

Scott slams a folder in front of me and grabs a chair, turning it around and sitting on it backwards across from me. I turn the page over, seeing an old photo of me with the words guilty stamped over my face in bold red ink.

I flip over, reading the next five pages which is a written account of what happened. The next part is for witnesses, and there is only one name with a brief statement about how he found me next to the bodies.

Scott places a finger over the guy's name. "I went to see this warden and he has never heard of you. Or this case." I suck in a deep breath of hope. "Flip the page."

I turn over to see a black and white photo of me that covers the whole page. I'm lying in the rubble with five dust-covered, bloody shapes mangled around me. The wardens. I stare at my face and then I notice the strap marks on my wrists and ankles. The bed I was lying on is just ash but the outline is there.

"This proves I was telling the truth," I whisper in shock, my palms turning clammy with excitement.

"Your whole case is bullshit. I've officially applied for a re-sentence...with your mum's assistance," Scott informs me and for a second I imagine walking out of here as a free woman.

I could have my name cleared and be back at Shadowborn Academy in no time.

Then I think of Gold, Luke, Axel, and my friend Memphis...I'd have to leave them all behind. How could I possibly do that?

"Is my mum really safe?" I ask, my hopeful voice giving away how much I needed to know she was all right.

Scott runs a hand through his hair, his eyes never leaving mine. "I can't tell you much, but after my brother was locked up for something he didn't do, I became fixated on making sure no one else became a victim. I've attended three hundred and twenty trials, and with about half of them, I found proof they didn't do what they were accused of."

"That's so amazing of you," I say honestly, and he waves a hand, like what he did for all those people it's nothing.

"Anyways, back to your mum. I knew of her, seen her a few times behind the stand but we have never formally met. I was surprised to have her contact me and tell me about this file and where to find it. Your mum told me she's safe and that there is a good reason why she's hiding."

The instant relief washes through me in waves. It's like a huge weight has been lifted off my shoulders and I can breathe again.

"She's alive, that's all that matters," I whisper, blowing out a long breath. "Thank you so much, Scott. Thank you!"

I throw myself into his arms and the chair scrapes against the tiles, threatening to topple us both over. Scott holds me to him, moving me slightly so my thighs fall on either side of his lap. The moment soon changes from laughter and fun to something far more. He softly slides his hands up my thighs, past my hips and to my waist. His thumbs lift my T-shirt up and grazes my skin above my jeans. A shiver slides through my body. Gods, this feels so good.

"When you're out, we're going on a date," he murmurs, and I'm too busy enjoying his touch to reply. "And the date is going to end with me buried so deep inside you that you will feel me for days after."

"Mm, that sounds wonderful. We could try it now if you want," I suggest slyly, making sure to rub myself against the hardness I feel under his jeans.

He groans, tightening his grip on my hips and tugging me to him. "Tease me as much as you want," he warns, his grumbling voice encouraging me to tease him some more. "But remember for every time you tease me, I'm going to make you pay for it."

"Are you counting?" I ask, biting down on my lip and he grins.

"From the second I saw you again, yes," he replies and lifts me off him. I all but pout as I sit back down and Scott grabs the exam paper he told me about, dropping it on my desk. "Now get to work, Miss Dawn. Teasing your teacher won't get you extra points."

"Dammit. My master plan has been discovered," I mutter and his laugh makes my cheeks warm and my heart beat all that much faster.

On my way to the mess hall, Luke pulls me aside.

"I want to show you somethin' real quick," he says, taking my hand and leading me down the corridor. He stops in front of the last window. "Look over there."

Raising a curious brow at him, I push onto my tiptoes and peer through the bars. From here I can see a beautiful oak tree bathed in sunlight and a man in brown fatigues planting a new headstone beside it. It's the headstone I asked Gold for, the one for Abbie and her brother—the one he had no obligation to fulfil and yet did. The little stone I've been working on is there, too, catching the afternoon sun.

Tears collect on my lashes, and I blink them away, smiling at Luke. "Thank you. I know you helped arrange that."

He shakes his head at me, turning back to the hall. "It was the least I could do. Now let's eat, jaybird."

CHAPTER TWENTY-THREE

Izora

THE GUST OF COOL AIR BLOWING OUT THE CANDLE on my nightstand is enough to wake me. I feel it sweeping over my body and lifting every hair, but it's more than just a draft. It tingles like dark magic circulating about me. I grab the knife I planted under my pillow and throw my legs over the bed. The scent doesn't belong to Luke, Gold, or Axel, which means they aren't welcome here.

"What do you want?" I demand, reaching for the panic button on the side of my nightstand. Luke said I should only use it in emergencies. Well, this is as good an emergency as any.

The only reply I get is a low, sinister chuckle. My room is shrouded in darkness, making it impossible to see, but the laugh definitely came from the window. I press the button and slip out of bed, clutching the knife in my hand. A tall figure steps out from the shadows and into the ribbons of moonlight bleeding through the bars.

"C-Coen..."

Another chuckle, this one with darker conviction. "Always so slow, you shadowborns."

He takes a step and I take one back towards the door. I'm not sure how long it'll take Luke to get here. Seconds, minutes, I don't know. I just hope it'll be soon because Coen clearly has use of his magic again despite his collar, and I'm willing to bet he plans on using it.

"Why are you here? Or have you come for your revenge?" I laugh despite the panic creeping into my body.

Coen laughs, too, but it holds a distinctive air of malice I know he's always felt for me.

"Maybe you're not as dumb as you fucking look," he says. "Things are about to change, Izora Dawn. Let's see if you're ready... Let's see if you survive this time."

He shadowlocates to my side in the blink of an eye, the shadows still clinging to his shoulders. I throw myself forward and aim for his jugular, but an abrupt pain grips hold of me. It runs down my legs like and I stumble back, glaring at the rush of blood seeping through my sweatpants. Coen disappears into thin air, leaving nothing but his laugh that fades into darkness and the unusual knife he slashed me with.

The pain swiftly turns into a searing agony and my vision blurs. No, no, no. I can't die like this. I hobble over to my bed and press the button repeatedly. Where the hell is Luke? Why isn't he here yet? The door opens slightly and relief floods my veins, but nobody comes in. Shrieks and screams fill the hallway outside. My heart races and clenches in my chest, my breathing constructing in my throat as I struggle to breathe.

I slowly inch my way over, wrapping my hand around the handle.

The second I do, a bright light blasts my eyes and then everything goes dark...

CHAPTER TWENTY-FOUR

Izora

TEARS AND ASH COAT MY LASHES WHEN I NEXT open them. I gaze up at the cracks in the ceiling above me in the flickering corridor. The ringing in my ears is deafening, and I close my eyes again, unable to keep them open.

When I come to, my hearing has returned and the ringing has vanished, but nothing but pain courses through my body. Inmates run past me lying on the floor. I'm surrounded by debris and ash that coats my lashes and creeps into my mouth. Everything is woozy and filled with pain. Something big is on fire nearby, and I'm dying, that much I know is for certain.

Another deafening bang shakes the walls around me, increasing the pain already tearing me asunder. Screams and cheers bellow in place of the eruption. I reach out and try to crawl to the wall, my throat clogged with fear and a rising sickness that threatens to purge from my mouth. Using what little strength I have, I use the wall to help myself stand, but my legs are out of commission, unable to support me. I slide down against the wall and close my eyes.

"Darling, no!"

My mother's screams carry to my ears, jolting me awake again. I barely manage to turn my head around now, but I do see my mother running down the corridor, her silvery blonde hair whipping in the air behind her. Gold appears out of nowhere. He picks me up off the floor and holds me to his chest, his forehead creased in alarm.

"How could you let anything happen to her?" my mother screams at him.

He stays silent as he looks down at me. At least I think he does... everything is blurry. So blurry and sore. I just want to close my eyes now.

"What the fuck happened?" Luke roars, shadowlocating to my side.

I lift my hand and feebly tap my leg where the cut is. Luke peels a magical dagger out from the shadows and cuts my jeans, revealing something that makes them all look nothing but fearful.

"Th-that b-b-ad, huh?" I manage to mutter but they are all staring at me in silence.

My mother bursts into tears but no one says anything.

I've never seen Mum cry before. Must be bad. Oh, god... gonna pass out again...

"Don't close your eyes. Look at me, jaybird," Luke whispers, tapping the side of my face.

My head rolls to the side but I manage to keep my eyes open, focusing on his face.

"The left wing has been blown up. That's where we get out."

"What should we do?" Luke asks in an unusually nervous voice.

Mother is still crying.

Why is she crying? Oh, yeah… I'm dying… I don't want to die.

"The fae must know of a cure. We go and beg them," Gold commands.

Finally, the siren, the fire, and everything makes sense now. This was all the fae's doing.

"King Ulric will help her," my mother whispers, cupping my cheek. "He would never turn her away."

"Why?" Luke voices what I wish I could, but we are already moving down a corridor and up a flight of stairs, and everything hurts so much that I'm struggling to breathe let alone focus.

"We will save you. Don't you fucking dare leave me, Izora," Gold whispers, pressing a kiss to my forehead, and I smile, despite everything.

But then Gold roars in pain and his hands abandon my body, letting me tumble down the stairs. I cry out, every jolt like red-hot daggers piercing my body, until I crash to the bottom step. Tears pool in my eyes as I hear more screams and shouts. I try to call out for my mother, for Gold and Luke, even Axel and Scott, but no words come out…and no one comes for me.

A strange acceptance fills my soul. The second it does, I start to relax and the pain almost drifts away. A blinding white light blasts into my eyes. I start to chuckle then, my pain completely gone now as the light gets brighter until I see the shape of someone emerging. The silhouette of a woman slowly comes into view, her blonde hair like spun gold, her pale skin as envious as much her curves are in her beautiful white gown. The flowing material is molded to her body with a long train puddling at her feet. Her eyes are the most captivating. They're like two kaleidoscopic pools of butterfly wings all captured into a pair of beautiful eyes.

"The time has come for us to meet. Many creatures have foreseen our friendship, Izora Dawn."

The woman's voice is light and yet firm, an alluring concoction that makes every syllable sound like she's whispering nothing but seductive sins.

"Who are you?" I ask and the strange urge to laugh still makes me giggle.

The woman giggles with me, leaning closer with a big smile. "We will fly together, you and I."

I laugh more with her, but I don't know why. Everything is just so funny. So strange. Wasn't I dying just a moment ago?

Her gaze turns serious for a moment. "I'm only human but I am a gift given to my ten lovers who are titans. My only power lies with them. I will need you to save them, dear Izora, but not yet. We will meet again but until then, you have my blessing."

"Blessing? What for? What's a titan?"

She slowly fades back into the darkness and tears fill my eyes as I watch her go. "A king of the gods. And when they awaken, soon, no one but us will be able to stop them."

CHAPTER TWENTY-FIVE

Izora

THE AIR TASTES ALMOST SWEET AS I WAKE UP, jolting from the chain attached to my ankle. The blood in my veins quickly freezes as I realise I'm not in my room… or anywhere that I recognise. White walls, white tiles, a single barred window and thick white bars like that of a cage surrounds me. I place my bare feet on the cold floor, shivering from the contact, and step forward. But then I notice my shadow from the sunlight pouring in through the window.

A shadow with wings.

I turn my head and all the air seems to leave my body when I see white, glittering wings fluttering behind me. I lift my hand to stroke them, and my fingertips vibrate with pure magic.

Light magic.

I rush to the bars, looking down an empty corridor

and flickering my gaze into the big open-cell before me. It's empty but I still shout for help.

"Hello! Is anyone there?"

Nobody answers, and I grip the bars tighter, an intense feeling of desperation filling me. I have a million questions and each of them starts with Gold once I find him.

How did he know my mother?

How and why was she even in the prison?

And the most important one of all: how am I alive?

I remember him holding me as I was dying and then I was falling down a flight of stairs. The most beautiful woman I'd ever seen came to me then. She spoke about titans and gods and gave me her blessing. I thought I died after she faded away. But now...now I'm here, with wings. Now I'm a light fae just like when this whole nightmare began.

"About time you woke up. They kept you sleepin' for a month," Luke's voice drifts to me.

I search the open cell for him, but it's not until he steps into the light do I see him. His skin is pale, his clothes are white like mine and there's a collar around his neck. His wings send me stumbling back in shock, even as Axel comes to his side and I see that he, too, has wings.

Whoever is in control here has turned everyone into a light faes.

"How?" I scarcely whisper the word, gripping the bars tightly. "Where is Gold?"

"Look out the window, Izora," Axel commands, nodding to the window of my cell.

I shakily step back and walk over. This can't really be happening, can it? I push up on my tiptoes just before my wings take over and lift my off the ground. I barely notice I'm flying, it feels so natural and painless to me, and that alone is terrifying. I look out the window at the breathtaking view of the Light Fae King's palace in the distance. Fae men and women fly around the city nestled below, their wings glittering in the bright sunlight.

By Selena, this is impossible…

And who is going to save me now?

TO BE CONTINUED…

New to the Shadowborn World? Buy the first book in Corvina Charles' journey at the elusive! *Shadowborn Academy!*

Excerpt from *Shadowborn Academy*
(Dark Fae Academy Series: Book One)

My fate is in the dark,
And my shadow there is real…

The darkness likes to play in this world.

It also likes to deceive.

In the Enchanted Forest, secrets thrive and one girl
desperately needs to find answers before it's too late.

That girl is Corvina Charles, a powerful Shadowborn—a
human who touched dark magic and became something
else.

Something dangerous.

At the age of eighteen, Corvina and her best friend are
swept away to the Shadowborn Academy, the one place
where magic and darkness coincide.

It's also where pupils go missing, teachers don't play by
any rules, the therapist is hot, and boys with dark magic
love to seduce your soul.

With death becoming a game at the academy that not
even the Dark or Light Fae seem capable of winning,

Corvina's love life should really be the last thing on her mind...especially when one of the boys just so happens to be her teacher!

Shadowborn Academy is a Dark Reverse Harem Paranormal Fae Romance for 18+. In this world, not even the shadows can be trusted...

CHAPTER ONE

Corvina

THE MOONLIGHT BLEEDING THROUGH THE TREES creates flickering shadows that dance around me. I should be afraid of them like all the other children are, but I'm not. These shadows are safe. They're not like the ones watching me from the treetops, waiting to snatch me off the ground.

No, these shadows are different.

They're my friends.

The faeries hiding in them follow me like they always do when I come into the Enchanted Forest. I can't see them but I can hear them giggling and whispering in my ear. They flick my dark curly hair over my shoulders and play with the ribbons on my light blue dress, then the frills of my white socks with the little bunny rabbits on them. It's their way of saying hello and it makes me giggle as I skip through the forest, humming to the song Mama always sings to me before I go to sleep.

Mama and Papa warned me not to follow these faeries. They said they're not like the rest and I'll be in deep trouble if I ever go out to play after dark. That's when the faeries come out. They sing to children like me and promise us things beyond our wildest dreams, but nobody ever sees them again once they follow the faeries into the forest. Mama said it's because they gobble them up for supper. I don't believe her. I mean, how horrible would that be? I don't think we taste very nice.

Pitch said the real reason the children don't come back is magical.

He told me that they grow wings and go to live with the faeries. He said I can do that, too, once I make my wish. I'm so excited. I can hear him singing to me and I start humming along to his favourite song, the one about the raven and the wishing well. I follow his voice, excited to play with him again and eat snacks and tell each other stories. No one else can see or hear Pitch apart from me and the faeries. Although we're the same age, he doesn't look like any of the boys from my village. He's extremely pale with glowing amber eyes and long ebony hair that sways around him like the shadows do in here. I know he's different and that's why I like him.

That's why I'm following him.

Now that it's my eighth birthday, Pitch is going to let me make a wish in the well he sings about. He says only special humans—the chosen ones—get to make a wish here. Sometimes he says funny things like that and I don't understand him. All I want is a pair of shiny blue shoes, the same ones as my dolly. Pitch says the faeries are going to give them to me, and then I'll finally have the same outfit as my little dolly.

The faeries guide me to the edge of a clearing which is bright from the moonlight shining down. I wave goodbye to them, even though I can't see where they are, then I continue humming and skipping after Pitch.

I can see him now, sitting on top of the well, and my heart soars as I race through the clearing. Once I reach the well, he lifts me onto the stone with him. It's wide enough that the two of us can stand together without falling into the hole.

"It's time to make your wish," he says, and my stomach fills with butterflies. "Are you ready to be born again?" I don't know what he means by that; I just want the lovely shoes. I nod anyway, and Pitch smiles at me. "Then close your eyes."

When I do this, I hold my breath, too excited to breathe.

My heart feels like it's going to burst out from my chest. I feel dizzy and sick and excited.

"Do you remember what we talked about?" Pitch asks quietly. "What you do once you make your wish? It's very important that you don't forget that part."

"I won't forget," I tell him firmly, peeking through my eyelashes. "Can I say it now? Can I make my wish?"

He giggles and lets go of my hand. "Go on, Corvina. Make your wish and make it count."

I let out an excited squeal, then I scrunch up my little face and think really hard because I don't want to mess this up.

—Hello faeries! Please can I have the same shoes as my dolly? You know, the sparkly blue shoes with the pretty bows on the silver buckles? I would like them very much. Thank you.—

With my wish uttered, I open my eyes. Pitch is gone just like he said he would be and I'm alone on the well. I look down into the tunnel of darkness stretching before me. A loose pebble falls away from the edge and drops into the well. It takes forever to splash through the water at the bottom, and I gulp, my palms turning sweaty against my dress.

For my wish to come true, I need to go down there.

Pitch said he'll be waiting for me and that the faeries will even give me wings so that I don't hurt myself. I'll be just like the other children who followed the faeries into the woods and lived happily ever after. Maybe I'll even be able to see my friends, Bella and Michael and Agnes.

We'll all be faeries together, like we used to talk about.

I turn around and spread my arms out like wings, smiling at the thought of seeing my friends from school again. Taking a deep breath and holding it in my chest, I close my eyes and fall down into the well, praying that Mama and Papa were wrong about the faeries, and about Pitch, the monster hiding under my bed…

Before I plunge to my death, I wake up with a gasp for air, crutching my thin bedsheets in my hands. Pitch wasn't waiting for me. There was nothing but pain and misery at the bottom of that stupid well and my innocent ass didn't know any better back then.

I fell into magical darkness, and as everyone here tells me, that's when I became a shadowborn.

But that's not the part that haunts me every night in my dreams. Oh, no. It's what happened after the pain and misery—after I drowned in all the magical water, my eight-year-old body absorbing it like it was sugar and I was a starving kid. When my heart started beating again and I opened my eyes, I lay floating on my back as the moon drew closer and closer to me. I remember crying and thinking I had been turned into a bug instead of a faery, but it was just the water healing my shattered bones and floating me up to the surface.

The second my feet touched the earth again, my power exploded and I destroyed everything in a five-mile radius, including all the houses and the people inside them.

Including my parents.

And the only living thing was me, covered in ash, lying on the forest floor as the sun rose into a blood-red sky.

Talk about a birthday to remember.

After that, I was picked up by the Shadow Wardens, protectors of the magical world, and thrown in a shadowborn foster home with all the other children that are like me. Only they didn't kill hundreds of people and not one of them in here see their powers like the curses really are.

"You having those dreams again?" Sage asks, sitting up on her bed next to me and staring at me, the moonlight highlighting her beige skin and curly pink hair that isn't at all messy even though she just woke up. Sage Millhouse is the only bit of this foster home that I've ever cared about and I'm certain it's the same way for her. We came here on the same day, two scared kids who wanted nothing more than to escape this hellhole and the new powers we have. Sage got her power the way most of the kids here did, by being bitten by a shadowborn in their animal state. One bite is enough to infuse any soul with shadow magic, and all it took for Sage was a bite from a fox in her garden.

The fox was never seen again, and Sage nearly died, only to survive and be taken from her parents to come and live here.

The foster home is full of those stories, and it's the main reason I don't talk about my past.

"Always."

It's all I need to say for Sage to get off her bed and head out of the room. I follow her, the old wooden floorboards creaking under my bare feet with each step. Sage holds the timber door open and we head outside into the garden. The cool air is refreshing for only a second before it's nothing but cold nipping at my skin.

"Ready?" I ask her as I stare up, the darkness and shadows comforting me like they always do.

Sage doesn't reply, though I'm unsurprised as she isn't one for words. That's why I like her. I watch her bright purple eyes as she disappears in a cloud of black smoke. The darkness. It's become a blanket of sorts to people like us. As the blackness fades away, there is nothing more than a hawk sitting on the ground, its lavender eyes staring up at me. I grin as I close my own silver eyes and do the next best thing in the world.

I let the darkness take me, creating me into something more.

Something so much better than I already am.

My body disappears into the darkness but my mind always stays, loving the comfort as I shift into a raven and follow Sage into the skies of Blackpool.

CHAPTER TWO

Corvina

"We should head back," Sage suggests around a spoonful of ice cream.

I watch the sea lap at the steps beside the shore and the sandbags lined at the top of them. The skies are grey, eerily so, like they can sense what a crap day this is going to be for us. The sea smells of salt and I can almost taste it over the bubblegum lollipop I've just finished off. Over the sounds of the waves, the seagulls make themselves known with loud squeaks, and in the distance, some children ride bikes down the front.

"Why? I have nothing to pack and neither do you. The wardens aren't coming until nightfall," I remind her. She eyes me carefully and I try to pick up on her emotions. Is she as nervous as me? Unlikely. The Shadowborn Academy is our next home, starting from tonight. We both have known we would attend this year, on the year we turn eighteen, since we aren't classed as kids anymore

The academy is meant to teach us control and endurance, to accept our new life and fit into their society of normal magics.

What if you don't want to fit in?

I asked our warden that once, and she laughed like it was the funniest thing in the world.

"They might not come for us at all. Wouldn't that be nice?" she replies, and I smirk at her, leaning back on the bench. I chuck the stick of my ice lolly in the bin and go back to people watching the streets.

I love people watching, and so does Sage. We have spent days on this bench, making up stories for random strangers we spot. Our stories are unlikely to be right, but it gives us an escape into a normal world—a world where our nightmares cannot reach us. We can almost pretend we're just two teenagers skipping school instead of what we really are.

"Do you think Keeper Maddox will miss us?" Sage asks, her voice dripping with humour.

The Light Warden runs our foster home and she's the fourth one since I came here, as all the others quit. No one likes looking after dozens of kids with shadow powers, and all of whom want their parents back. These poor wardens would literally prefer any other assignment in the magics world. It's depressing, but Keeper Maddox isn't the worst of the lot.

"I doubt she will even notice us leave. She prefers the younger ones," I reply.

They're easier to control.

As for me and Sage?

We're damaged goods and a waste of air. Or so we've been told by previous wardens. Sometimes late at night, when my demons catch up with me, I almost believe them.

"And you have your book? In the name of Selena, do not forget that book, child," Keeper Maddox warns me later that day, giving my opened trunk an assessing once over. Spotting the old, tattered book beside my trunk, she nods. "Thank the Gods. You mustn't forget it. Always have your book with you—"

"—from the instant you enter the forest," I tersely interject, having endured this spiel many times before now. "The book is our bible. We get it, Miss Maddox."

We've had no choice but to.

I've read the *Book of Zorya* a million times already. I don't know why she'd think we'd leave here without it. It's practically the map to our new home. A home neither of us wants to be part of.

Well, Sage says she doesn't, but I have a sneaky suspicion she's excited to use magic beyond the mediocre level we were taught here. The wardens never wanted us to learn more than needed since we were supposed to be part of the mortal world.

The mortal world.

After ten years, it still feels odd to not be quite human anymore. I had human parents, lived in a human village, before I was…changed. Now I'm just a shadowborn, and

I must go to this academy to learn the tricks of the trade. Part of me should at least feel excited, but I'm not. I'm more terrified than anything else. The last time I entered the Enchanted Forest, my whole world was taken from me.

"Very well, then," Maddox starts, gesturing to my trunk. "Your luggage should arrive at the academy by the time you arrive. Why don't you go stand outside with the others?"

She leaves without waiting for a reply.

I look out the window above what used to be my rickety bed. Sage is sitting on her tire swing in the back garden, looking down at Little Nessa's grave. She was a kid who used to stay here before she lost control of her power. Sage and I shared a room with her, and we always managed to calm her down when she had nightmares. But that night we went out for a fly, and when we came back, they were carrying Nessa's small body out. I remember looking at her and thinking how peaceful she looked, as if she were just sleeping. But that's the thing with shadowborns. Our magic feeds off the darkness residing within us, and often it takes over.

Our fears, our heartaches, our pain… anything that affects us negatively, the magic pulsing through our veins latches on to them and grows stronger with every fruitless effort we make to fight them.

Some of us learn to control our dark sides, at least for a while. Others, like Nessa, never stand a chance from the moment they were turned into a shadowborn. This is why the academy exists: to teach magics like me how to accept our demons instead of hiding from them. Running, avoiding, suppressing, all these things merely worsen our condition. I learned that a long time ago, and I managed to accept my demons.

The darkest one of all is named Pitch, and he's also my shadow.

Speaking of the devil, which he might be for all I know, Pitch doesn't always talk to me. I guess he doesn't really need to. His thoughts are my fears and my fears are his thoughts now. No matter where he goes, I can always sense him without looking. It's inherent, not because I want it to be, but because we're soul mates.

Literally.

The night that I died, I was the only light left within his swirling darkness, and he latched on to me by tethering my soul to his so we could both stay alive. He never meant for either of us to suffer and die. Only a child himself, he merely wanted to grant my birthday wish.

I never quite bought that either in the beginning. But despite all the anger and pain I felt towards him for many years later, I've come to accept that without him, without his darkness nestled around my heart, my soul would be incomplete. He's a part of me whether I want him to be or not, and any time we're apart, a gut-wrenching longing takes over me, and it burns right through to my core.

I turn back, seeing a shadow of a figure in the corner of the room, sitting on an empty bed. Sometimes Pitch looks like a man with broad shoulders, thick black hair, and alluring amber eyes. And sometimes, like this, he is just a shadow that blinks away before I can ask why he's even here.

Clearing my throat, I leave and head down the corridor, my navy boots announcing every footstep in the dark, dimly lit hallway. Pushing the door open, I step out into the moonlight as Sage stands and turns to me, clutching her copy of the *Book of Zorya* in her hands. This is how I know she's excited to go to the academy—she's forever reading that damn book.

"Is it time?" she asks, and I simply nod. Hooking her arm in mine, we leave the garden and head to the front of the house. We walk outside, sitting on the brick wall, watching the stars in the sky.

"They say it's so dark in the enchanted forest, and unless you have the blessing of the sun and moon, you can't see where you walk," she half-jokes, but I can tell she is nervous.

I roll my eyes at her. It can't be that bad. "You need to stop reading that book. Wait and see. We will be there soon."

She opens her book and starts reading, ignoring me completely.

"In the beginning, Aphrodite and Persephone decided to create a magical forest for all manner of creatures. They appeared in their natural form, unearthly beautiful and fae-like, and brought with them their favourite stars—the Morning Star and the Evening Star. They each placed them in the sky, and one became the sun and the other the moon," she reads out, her voice being carried by the wind to poor unsuspecting humans who don't want to hear a fairy tale like this.

A fairytale that quickly became a nightmare.

"I know, I know. Then monsters came to the forest. Blah, blah, blah," I drone but she ignores me once more and carries on reading.

"Aphrodite became known as Danica, Goddess of the Sun, and she created the Throne of Helios where she would reign over her part of the forest. Persephone became Selena, Goddess of the Moon, and she created the Throne of Luna, again where she would rule her half of the forest. To their kingdoms, they became known as the Zorya Sisters..." She stops, turning the page and pausing in whatever she's reading.

"I've heard the thrones are cursed and that's why all the royal fae are crackers," I whisper to her. Keeper Maddox and every keeper I've met talk like fae are these holy creatures and to speak badly about them is as forbidden as murder.

"Rumours, all rumours, Corvina," she sighs, snapping the book shut. "Aren't you excited to see a fae student? They're meant to be very alluring and beautiful."

Alluring and beautiful is exactly how I would describe Pitch.

But often those things just hide a person's true nature like a cloud of smoke.

When I finally focus on Sage, her all too knowing eyes are watching me closely. "I know you're scared. It's okay to admit it to me, Corvina."

"Since I became a shadowborn, I've been scared,

Sage, but I've learnt that running from it only gives the fear more power. It's better to face the darkness than run from it because one thing is for damn sure..." I pause as I see something coming down the road. "In our world, the darkness never lets you go."

Appendix I—LOCATIONS
(as mentioned in the book)

Zorya Kingdom

THRONE OF LUNA
Capital City: LUNA
Ruler: Queen Narah

DEADLANDS
Inhabits: Cimmerians, Draugers, Deserters, Bandits

THE BLACK HARBOUR

THE WISHING WELL

SKULL CAVE
aka Howling Hollow Cave, Statue of Aeon

THE GORGON LAKE

FAERIE POOLS

DEVIL'S DROP

SHADOWBORN ACADEMY

SHADOWBORN PRISON

DRACONIA
Capital City: Emeria

Ruler: King Cyrus, Naraah's brother
Queen Valessia
Prince Drusus
Prince Draco
Prince Drakon
Princess Kaida

ZORYA INN

Helios Kingdom

THRONE OF HELIOS
Capital City: VASILI
Ruler: King Ulric
Princess Evangelina

LAKE LUMEN

HELIOS ACADEMY

AURORA BAY

PEGASUS TAVERN

FAERIE POOLS

KYLLAROS
Ruler: Chiron
Prince Elias

Appendix II—Prison Layout

GROUND FLOOR
Entrance/Security
Armories
Processing Room
Visiting Centre
Wardens' Staffroom
Education
Therapist
Library

FIRST FLOOR
Girl's Wing > showers, leisure area
Boy's Wing > showers, leisure area
Mess Hall

SECOND FLOOR
Solitary Confinement
Training Room
Green Room

THIRD FLOOR
Blood Trials Arena
Infirmary
Morgue
Laboratory

THE TOWER
(located on the third floor, upper left)
Governor's chamber
Izora's new cell/room
Staff quarters

Appendix III—Characters

INMATES
Izora Dawn, arena trainer
Axel, trainer, chef
Memphis, arena trainer
Coen, arena pack alpha
Tyler, arena pack beta
Janis Roth, Blood Trials committee member
Sharon Roth, Blood Trials committee member
Abigail
Kenneth, Abigail's brother, deceased

STAFF
Zavier Gold, Governor of Shadowborn Prison
Shadow Warden (Derek) Luke, Izora's Guard
Lieutenant Warden (Nathaniel) Kyle, Blood Trials
Enforcer, Luke's uncle
Gage Michaels, Therapist, also teaches at Shadowborn
Academy
Scott Mune, Education Teacher, also teaches at
Shadowborn Academy
Doctor Frank, Infirmary

OTHERS
High Warden (Athena) Greene, Izora's mother
High Warden (Ezekiel) Greene, Izora's step-father
Willow Greene, Izora's step-sister
Emma Greene, Ezekiel's former wife, Izora's deceased
nanny
Corvina Charles, Izora's friend, Shadowborn Academy
student

GODS & GODDESSES
Selena, Goddess of the Moon, Persephone
Danica, Goddess of the Sun, Aphrodite

OTHER GODS
(not featured in this book yet)
Hades, God of Darkness
Ares, God of War
Aeon, God of Life
Eris, Goddess of Chaos and Discord

Appendix iv—Warden Ranks

Grand Wardens—royal advisors, supreme judges, head of the High Table, the most powerful of all the wardens

High Wardens—member of the High Table that govern certain fractions of the forest and human world (like mayors)

Shadow Wardens—law enforcers, highly trained and skilled, powerful

Junior Wardens—still powerful, will advance up to a Shadow Warden

Keepers—protectors of Shadowborns and magic users, never really advance

APPENDIX V—THE BOOK OF ZORYA
(how the Enchanted Forest came to be)

In the beginning…

Aphrodite and Persephone decided to create a magical forest for all manners of creatures. They appeared in their natural form, unearthly beautiful and fae-like, and brought with them their favourite stars—the Morning Star and the Evening Star. They each placed them in the sky, and one became the sun and the other the moon.

Aphrodite became known as Danica, Goddess of the Sun, and she created the Throne of Helios where she would reign over her part of the forest.

Persephone became Selena, Goddess of the Moon, and she created the Throne of Luna, again where she would rule her half of the forest. To their kingdoms, they became known as the Zorya Sisters.

As the Almighty Goddess of the Moon, Selena, walked through the forest at twilight, admiring her many creations, she came across a shard of glass gleaming on the forest floor. She used this to create the Fountain of Mene which allowed her to see whatever her heart most desired, and to guide her down whichever path she sought in darkness. Selena often used it to see her husband Hades and their children.

The Dark God, Hades, used this fountain to send her a cloak of darkness on their anniversary, which Selena wove it into a blanket of stars that became known as the night sky. Now the moon had stars, and Selena told her people to use them as guides and sources of light within the darkness, for neither of them should be feared since they cannot exist without the other; just like how Selena's kingdom cannot exist without Danica's.

Many decades later, a strange presence crept into the forest. Eris, Persphone's half-sister, had grown envious of this Selena and Danica and she planned to spoil their New World.

First, she unleashed monsters into the forest.

Darkness.

The creatures of dark spread like wildfire, breeding chaos everywhere and anywhere they could. Danica tried to chase them back whence they came, but Selena pitied and grew to love them. Some even became her loyal servants. While she became occupied with her new settlers, Eris sent Danica the Golden Apple of Discord, a feigned gift from Ares, which poisoned her.

Hearing of her sister's illness, Selena rushed to her side. Nothing could be done to save Danica. Eris watched from the shadows as Danica's light faded and her sun waned.

But then Selena ripped out her own heart and pressed it into Danica's chest. This allowed Danica to live, but Selena faded and died in Danica's arms, before she joined the stars in the sky, and because of her sacrifice, she became one with the Evening Star and the Moon.

When Hades learned of what happened, his anger shook the realms. He used the fountain as a portal and managed to kill Eris, but without his wife to bring out the good in him, Hades' grief drove him to insanity. He partnered up with Ambrose, the God of Life, and they waged war on the kingdoms. Hades killed Eris, but now that Danica had her powers and her sisters, she was able to severely injure him so much that he had to retreat back to the underworld and was stripped of his ability to return.

Peace settled among the forest for a time, and Danica gave the Throne of Luna to Ares, who was quick to succumb to the allure of darkness and he became the first Dark Fae—Queen Narah's four-times great-grandfather.

About
G. Bailey

G. Bailey is a *USA Today* bestselling author of books that are filled with everything from dragons to pirates. Plus, fantasy worlds and breath-taking adventures. Oh, and some swoon-worthy men that no girl could forget. G. Bailey is from the very rainy U.K. where she lives with her husband, two children and three cheeky dogs. And, of course, the characters in her head that never really leave her, even as she writes them down for the world to read!

About me?
I love tea. (Maybe a little obsessed but what Brit isn't?)
Chocolate and Harry Potter marathons are my jam.
I own way too many notebooks and random pens.

Please feel free say hello on here or head over to Facebook to join G. Bailey's group, Bailey's Pack (www.facebook.com/groups/BaileysPack)! (Where you can find exclusive teasers, random giveaways and sneak peeks of new books on the way!)

About
Scarlett Snow

Scarlett Snow comes from a big family in a small Scottish town and has always strived to prove that if you are passionate about something, no one can stop you from chasing your dreams. She lives with her wolf dog and kitties and is unashamedly addicted to coffee.

If you'd like to join her newsletter to be kept updated on her books, you can do so here: www.scarlett.katzesnow. com

Facebook Reader's Group:
www.facebook.com/groups/scarlettscoven

Facebook Page: www.facebook.com/authorscarlettsnow

OTHER BOOKS BY SCARLETT

Amazon:
www.amazon.com/Scarlett-Snow/e/B07NKFPSKN

Non-Amazon Book: https://payhip.com/b/K8Mr

Scarlett also writes under Katze Snow
(Dark M/M Books):
www.amazon.com/Katze-Snow/e/B01M0GTAED